In the 1980s I was living in [...] the news that a mass murd[...] lived three streets away. Onl[...] victims had even been reported missing; he had been found out by his inability to adequately dispose of the bodies in his basement flat. Commuters experienced a traffic jam that morning as motorists slowed to look at the house where it all occurred. The following day, life in N10 went on as usual.

This book celebrates a world where this is possible;our world, which in the same breath can be both banal and surreal.

I am indebted to the works of Noam Chomsky, Edward S Herman, Ann Gurton and Jon Boorstin for the media and film theory that underpins this novel.

THE DEATH OF ME

THE DEATH OF ME

by

Paul Vincent

CENTRAL PUBLISHING LIMITED.
West Yorkshire

Paperback ISBN 1 903970 60 1

**Published
by**

Central Publishing Limited.
Royd Street Offices
Milnsbridge
Huddersfield
West Yorkshire
HD3 4QY

www.centralpublishing.co.uk

The Death Of Me

RAY

I'm sitting in an unremarkable bar 1200 miles from home and a stranger walks up to my table and addresses me by name. He could be the police. He could have rung the registration of my rig through, but it is unlikely. He is well dressed and he wants to say something and I know I won't want to hear it.

He tells me about my life. He tells me about the journeys I make to and from England. He tells me about the bankruptcy I had two years before. As he talks I become more aware of the heat. It must be in the hundreds and I'm not sure I can hear or think.

He's not asked me for anything, but he will. He has an accent, but he's probably not Spanish. I listen to his speech but not to what he's saying. He could be British. Second generation something.

He notices a waiter clear up a nearby table and asks him for two more coffees. I don't drink coffee.

I think, *My stranger doesn't know this. He knows about my life but he doesn't know what I drink.*

My stranger keeps smiling. He wants me to keep eye contact with him. Laugh when he laughs. I hate him. I check myself for racism.

No, it's simply that he's an arsehole.

I look to see if anyone is witnessing us. If they were called upon, would they remember this man talking to me? The restaurant looks overstaffed, but nothing is getting done. There are four waitresses at the bar sorting out one bill between them. They are oblivious to us. I turn my attention back to the man in front of me.

'But your wife,' he is saying, 'she had your truck in her name. Perhaps you knew that your business was going under?'

I shake my head.

'So now you're a truck driver.'

That much was obvious.

'All I am saying is that you park your truck as usual. When you are in Spain you ring this number and you say that you are here. Just like if you were visiting a friend. I can be your friend.'

I doubt it.

'It is worth five thousand pounds a trip. Four trips a year...'

You would first have to leave it empty for a day. Maybe just overnight. But that would just be the one time.'

I assume he is talking about drugs but no matter how I conjure his words they don't add up. It's some other cargo, but I don't want to ask what.

He takes a piece of paper from his pocket. It already has something written on it. He folds it over. The business section of this meeting is done.

He looks pleased. He relaxes. I now see that up to this moment he has been nervous. He smiles as if we had always known each other, always enjoyed each other's company.

He looks out of the window and decides to talk about Catalonia and its history. I start thinking that he is mannered and educated. He refers to 'my land' and goes further and further back in history. It seems to be important to him. He talks about the Aragon-Catalonia kingdom and a leader in the ninth century called Wilfred the Shaggy.

I say, 'What? You specialise in surreal conversation or something?' then, 'well we did have an Ethelred the Unready,' and I hate myself for wanting to make him feel at ease.

He talks about Ethelred and the Danish king Sweyn who deposed him. He cares little about my life, but he wants to impress me.

I didn't graduate in trafficking. I studied European History at Kings College, London. But after university I was grateful for any job, and one thing led to another. You know how you fall into a career.

Definitely.

#

If I have two defining traits it's that I'm a cartoonist and I'm lazy. Needless to say, they're not in that order.

My idea of perfect happiness would be a boss to tell me what to do, and a PA to do it. It's so not going to happen.

Because I'm lazy I have to do an awful lot of work. If I got my arse into gear I would be able to make a living from my cartoons but instead I am stuck in my dead end job working my arse off for a short staffed local paper, The Reapham Gazette. I write at least half the stories, get no respect and barely a credit, while my editor gets wined and dined and feted. He does let me print any relevant cartoons I draw, and I'm still young enough at 23 to get a thrill from that.

As far as I'm concerned, the story began with Matt Mann and Justine Dolly. They were out in the middle of a field in the Fens copping off, or their approximation of it.

Matt is a complete soap dodger: a greasy gnome of a thing with a lot of hair. When drawing him I opt for black Indian ink and a dip pen. Bold, black lines where the hair sprouts from his cheeks and falls in matted greasy clumps. Plenty of white, blank paper would be left on his hair to intimate the shine in it from all the grease. Because he is short, I would give him child like proportions. When drawing an adult, the height of the head should take up a sixth or seventh of the total height, but in

Matt's case his head would make up a full quarter of his five foot or so.

I draw everyone around here, regardless of whether or not they get in the local paper. It's something to do to make sure my real work piles up nicely.

On the night in question Justine was having to be careful with Matt because he'd just had a tattoo done on his scrotum. It read, 'Warning May Contain Nuts,' but they ran out of skin so the 'uts' got lost round the corner and was hiding in the undergrowth somewhere. I'm not sure I believe the latter bit of the story, but I'm not going to be looking for myself, so I guess I'll never know. So to keep going, Matt's tattoo was so new it had the cling film still on it that the tattooist recommended. He didn't have proper surgical tape to keep it in place, so he'd used gaffer tape instead. I would have loved to have been there when he tried to pull it off.

Justine was giving him a blowjob. Now Justine has a big mouth and tongue so when I drew this I copied those two features from Pete Sampras. So imagine Pete Sampras doing the blowjob with big lollopy tongue actions and you've got the idea.

The impediments to Justine and Matt's romance were the traditional ones of poverty and parental disapproval. Justine's parents had forbidden her to see Matt. Full stop. So she would tell her little brother which field she was in and then put her knickers high up on an ear of wheat where he could see. That way if she needed to go home in a hurry, her brother could find her.

The Dolly sisters were harmless enough. The one that Matt went out with never looked up. It was like her neck was cricked down, or her chin is stuck to her chest with glue. I always have to draw her slightly from above, otherwise you miss the joke with her. Her eyes sort of flicker all the time as though you were just about to shout at her: I do a kind of double pupil for that.

She always wore a summer dress that was too short for her, which I drew as a simple triangle with two stick-like knobbly white legs dangling out the bottom. The legs never quite touch the ground and always have bruises and cold veins on them.

They were called the Dolly Sisters because the two of them pushed prams around the town - although again I've never seen this, so it probably isn't true. They just walk side by side both pushing their prams and there are dolls in the prams. These women are 25 for heaven's sake. And then often each side of them walk their two boyfriends. Matt has all these lairy love bites all over his neck. Black and red and sometimes it looks swollen. Basically he's just really proud of the fact that he has sex.

So Justine and Matt were getting down to it in the middle of a field and it was getting dark, when they heard noises and saw lights. Matt looked up over the wheat and discovered they were surrounded by aliens. Twenty, thirty, forty aliens. Big Roswell eyes, black gowns and a language no one understood. Matt panicked. Justine panicked more. She couldn't actually see what was happening because of her neck thing, but she picked up on Matt's unease and emitted huge, undulating, only-dogs-can-hear-you shrieks. When Matt panics he sort of hops up and down.

So that's the scene. It made no difference to the aliens. They kept making what we now know were crop circles. Huge spiralling shapes. Chanting songs from their planet. The spirals got narrower, and the untrodden section of wheat in which Justine and Matt were hiding was becoming a smaller and smaller patch in the middle. Eventually it got too much for them and they had to dash for it through the wheat and through the aliens: cartoon Y fronts down around his hairy little ankles.

The caption would be something like, 'Justine reflected that perhaps the Earth had moved after all.'

Of course, as a news story it all ended up on my desk, which is where I came in.

We did the love thing but not the couples thing.

If it were a film, it could have had a clumsy beginning: I would have to show, not tell.

My face appears through the curtains, looking down the street.

I go to the kitchen and look at the outsized clock on the wall. The second hand clicks up to the twelve at exactly that moment. Eight o'clock.

My face appears at the window again, looking right and left. It's a sash window, set in a decent sized Victorian property. This man is tasteful, he wears tasteful clothes.

The kitchen clock is shown again. Eight ten.

I mutter audibly, 'She's not turning up, she hates me.'

Only the mad and people in films voice their thoughts to the degree I am going to.

We see the clock again. Eight twenty.

'I hate her,' I say.

Eight thirty.

'How dare she look so nonchalant cycling down the middle of the street. Not even fast.'

I watch her for a while. Obviously the love interest, but in an art house kind of way. The young Juliette Binoche. Elusive and dark. She has a sit up and beg bike. She's smiling to herself, not knowing she's being watched.

'If I run back to the kitchen now I might not look so pathetically eager,' I say to myself in a self deprecating Hugh Grant style.

Still an art house film, but probably a romantic comedy too.

She lets herself in.

'I let myself in,' she calls down the hall. 'I hope you don't mind.'

'I love that you feel at home here,' I call back.

I put on thin surgical gloves.

In the kitchen, we're aware of music playing. Basement Jaxx. Chrissie walks in. She appears to be watching her shoes as she walks. She looks up and sees me, and pulls a smile.

We hug forever.

'You're wearing gloves,' she says.

'You told me to,' I reply.

'You're cutting onions?'

'You said that if I cut onions or chillies and I think I shall be wanking your clit, I should wear gloves or it would irritate you.'

I tell her news. I look excited and talk too much. I get the vodka from the freezer. She stands in the middle of the kitchen and throws her head from left to right listening and dancing to the music, all black hair, elbows and wedgy shoes.

She says, 'Men are so cold and calculating. They don't fall in love like we do.'

'You know me too well,' I say.

She gets herself another vodka and leaves the bottle out and I'm suddenly awkward.

The bottle forms a frosting of ice on the outside.

She starts to laugh, probably at me, but I laugh too.

There'd be a need for a narrator at this point, and let's face it no one likes narrators, even though in this case it would be my voice that's going over.

The narrator would say something like, 'The night the Monkey on a Stick held us up with a shotgun, Chrissie wasn't there at all. She said she might come, which meant she wouldn't, so I'd laid six for dinner.'

We were still in the house we'd previously established. A group of friends eating dinner. Some of us looked stoned, most were drunk, and everyone was very talkative in the way that long-standing friends are. Everyone was wearing contrasting colours; colours that weren't fashionable at the time.

Helen had just been to the cinema to see Bridget Jones.

'Have you noticed in these Romantic Comedies,' she said, 'that the lover usually has a group of cute friends who are barely given a story line.'

'It allows the protagonist to explain the obstacles the lovers are having to jump over, for the benefit of the viewer,' said Lisa.

'In real life,' I said, 'most really sizzling love is actually about sex, and your group of cute friends aren't going to want to hear the details.'

Someone countered by mentioning Sex and the City. It was now obvious to the casual observer that here was a group of friends who could drone for hours on the subject of films.

At the other end of the dinner table Sean was taking off his clothes. Lisa, to his right was taking off her dress for him to wear. She had put on a T-shirt and was wiggling her dress down and passing it over. Sean wasn't wearing underwear, so he was stark bollock naked. Lisa was a size twelve, maybe fourteen, and Sean was considerably bigger. It was all so in character that people barely noticed him.

Helen was now telling us a story. She was saying that Gabby's son had taught hers to wank.

'But they don't call it wanking. Tom showed him how to

make his willy explode. Of course if it really did explode, that would be a trick he could only do once.'

Gabby listened. Her head cocked to one side. An emaciated body. Big teeth. Some sort of eating disorder no one mentions.

Alan mumbled something but he was in no fit state to hold a conversation. He was looking at the remains of his dessert.

Then he was audible. 'I don't know why it's called passion fruit, it hasn't got even a whiff of cheese or fish about it,' he said.

A few of us turned our heads and laughed. Sean was pulling the dress up and down over his outsized arse. His nipples looked reedy through the fabric, but quite good. He swayed in a kind of dance to the music that played: Fiona Apple. Fiona Apple was American and had a piano. She was very angry about something.

Sean was explaining his foolproof theories for film criticism based on hairstyle. If Brad Pitt had blond hair it was a crap film; if he had dark hair it was good. If Jeff Bridges had long hair it was a crap film, if he had short hair it was great, or the other way round. He wasn't sure.

'And don't get me started on numerical significance in the cinema,' he said with a weak smile that either denoted bliss or a need to throw up.

'If there is a seven in the title it's great,' he said, 'if there's a nine it's awful. Seven, The Magnificent Seven, The Seventh Seal.'

'Seven Brides For Seven Brothers,' added someone.

'Nine,' continued Sean, 'Nine and A Half Weeks, 1941, 9 to 5, Nine Months. See?'

'Nineotchka,' I said, looking round for a laugh that plainly wasn't going to arrive.

Gabby mumbled that she liked 9 to 5. When no one agreed she looked despondent.

'Come and dance,' said Sean.

Gabby got up and danced with him.

Time passed. I was standing and doing a mock speech, talking about us as friends. It showed my romantic side. I told my friends that we were good people, fun people. We had escaped to our late thirties, early forties, and we still enjoyed ourselves. Perhaps our fun was quietly desperate - someone laughed at that - if we went clubbing we had to go en masse to avoid looking sad. We still poured off to the cinema, to new restaurants, or to see a band, just as we had always done, but nowadays we went to the theatre as well. We still had a good feel for music but we were happy to listen to Mark and Lard. We figured that if it was okay for Lard to graduate from playing in The Fall to playing Madonna, then it was alright for us too. Towards the end of my speech we pan back to reveal the fact that my fellow diners had long since lost interest.

I was distracted by a slight noise from the kitchen.

I announced, 'I'm going to get some more wine and put on the coffee.'

In the kitchen, the French window was broken and there was a hand fumbling through the pane to unlock it. I hung in the hallway and watched.

When the man entered the room, I stepped forward at the same time. We simply stood looking at each other for a while.

I became aware of a small light over the cooker hood, as if someone had just turned it on. The man stood, lit on one side: his right shoulder in yellow, his left barely visible. His clothing, his dark T-shirt, undulated slightly in a draft.

He kept trying to start a sentence. His face implied that he would be able to come up with a plausible reason for breaking the window and standing in my kitchen.

'I... . It's just that...'

'Yes?' I asked.

'I need... .'

A pause.

'I need to see Christine.'

I raised my head involuntarily, surprised to hear Chrissie's name.

The man moved further into the light. He was about 20 and looked like a monkey on a stick. When he moved, all his limbs moved at once, as though he were automated. He was very short, had long black hair and a long straggly greasy beard that sprouted from just below his eyes. He obviously didn't trim his hair or wash it in any shape or form. That is, in any shape or form that wasn't long and greasy. His hair parted on each side at the bottom to fall either side of his shoulders. When he talked, his teeth were thick with soft yellow curd. When I told someone later about the experience I mentioned that he reeked of biscuits and earth. It's a smell you sometimes come across in chronically unwashed children. They joked that only a dentist, like me, would have noticed the teeth though.

This little man then scuttled out of the door and into the darkness. He returned with a farmer's shotgun.

'I need to see Christine. Now,' he said.

He shuffled towards me, the barrel at chest height.

I brought my arms out sideways.

I said, 'Hey.' It showed confidence. It showed I felt he didn't have the nerve to pull the trigger.

He asked again where Chrissie was and eventually I explained that we would have to walk through the house together and that we had guests. This made no sense, of course, but it's what happened.

He had a barely perceptible twitch about his face. A tic. He now seemed too nervous to even speak. He nodded.

We walked down the corridor together. I led; he was doing a shuffle behind me. After a few steps my body would lurch forward, stumble, as if trying out the concept of running fast.

Then I was running down the corridor. I was pelting down it. My arms were raised to shoulder height.

I was at the banister. I put one hand out and swung round it. It felt like slow motion.

There was a noise of a bang or perhaps just a stumble, but I was already round the corner.

There was another noise; a whoosh or swirl very close to my right ear, but unidentifiable and it didn't impede me.

I made it to the dining room. Lisa looked up at me, straight into my eyes. I banged the door shut and then reached for a chair to wedge against it. There was no noise of the Monkey on a Stick running down the corridor, but within an instant I could see the door moving rhythmically where he was pushing it.

I told everyone we needed to barricade the door. But they just looked at me and didn't move at all.

The door kept pushing against me and I looked terrified. When it stopped pushing against me, I froze. I focussed on the door. A stripped pine Victorian door with black porcelain finger plates. There was no sound, no movement.

I said, 'Move the table against the door. Please. Please move the table against the door. There is someone with a gun. I am telling you there is someone with a gun.'

Helen started taking some of the glasses and bottles off the table so that if we were going to be shot at least there wouldn't be wine stains on the carpet.

Alan was barely awake, so when the table was moved he was left in his chair swaying a little. Sean, still wearing the black Lycra dress, helped push.

'Now if we stay at the other end of the table to keep it pushed in place,' I said. 'Has anyone got a mobile to call the police?'

Someone pointed out that pushing against the table kept us in the firing line.

So the tableau was formed by anorexic Helen, Gabbie, Sean in the black dress, Lisa naked apart from a T-shirt and me all pushing against the table, while Alan sat bolt upright, apparently asleep.

Fiona Apple sang from the stereo that she'd 'acquired quite a taste for a well-made mistake.' Then the central panel of the door splintered open. Some of us ducked down and some moved sideways and I found myself crouching and looking at Helen who was beside me breathing hard in that way that happens when you're trying to stay silent.

We were in the same position, waiting. Seeing us waiting for such a long time without movement, meant that something would happen. This was not the end of the scene. I looked towards the windows. I focussed, in the way drunks do, on the window locks.

'Where are the keys to the window locks?' I said to no one in particular.

Our heads turned in unison towards the window. In the same moment the glass shattered. It wasn't a gunshot. There was the fleeting sight of a gun butt through the hole in the window. We could just make out the Monkey on a Stick in the darkness outside.

A pause again, a pause long enough to make us jump when the Monkey on a Stick leant through the hole in the glass. He was looking for bolts to undo.

Then we knew the situation had turned around. It seemed the Monkey on a Stick felt he had to undo the bottom bolts to get in and was taking too long doing it. He leaned through the glass and bent forward. He still couldn't quite reach the bolts so he bent further, but they were still just beyond him. He should, of course, have broken the glass a second time further down and reached through there. He kept struggling, leaning over the glass, and because he was only wearing a T-shirt he was cutting himself in a line from one side of his stomach to the other. There was blood beginning to run down the window, but he was fixed on his task.

We watched transfixed as two lines of thick blood moved down the glass, vivid red in the artificial light.

The lines of blood were slow at first but they became thicker and faster as he kept pushing himself down, grinding himself from left to right over the glass. The blood reached the bottom of the window frame, clumping up on the wooden beading below.

Sean, in his black dress, put his hand hard on the Monkey's head forcing him down over the glass, holding him firm.

Someone behind me was talking on their mobile phone to the police.

RAY

To stave off the boredom of driving, I play games. I read an English newspaper or I listen to the radio news. I try to categorise the information. I remember three pieces of it, one from each of my categories, then test myself later to see if I can recall them.

My categories are political, show business and human interest. Any paper will do, but I try to get the Telegraph because it has the most news in it. It's good on politics but also good at the smaller human interest stories that add spice to a paper.

Today a country is waging war over a piece of desert land where nothing can grow. The people who live there want to be autonomous.

Some starlet falls out of her dress at a premier; some of the journalists miss it, so she does it again.

Two nurses are suspended from a British hospital. They were caught squeezing the spots on patients' faces while they were under general anaesthetic.

It is an average day for news, and easy enough to memorise: Middle East war, topless starlet, acne, or as the tabloids would probably say, 'NHS introduce spot checks.'

After fifty miles, or just before the next newsbreak, I have to recall my three news stories. It helps keep my brain going and gives me something to do.

I've become quite obsessive about the news items. I'm not sure why. I am a lonely man and I think perhaps it forms a link for me to England; a link to my previous life where I'd sit at the kitchen table and read the paper every day. In fact I hate it. I hate that I have to do such petty things to pass my time. I often despise the items themselves, especially the show business stories. But it's like having an itch to scratch. I can't resist doing it. And if I don't do it, I just dwell on my life and the past. I re-run it, re-write it, bury bits, nurse grudges; obsess. I shouldn't be left alone with myself.

I read the paper in the cab. I select my three stories then climb out and onto the road. I've got an appointment with the Spanish police.

The policeman I see looks assured. He's important. It's not so reassuring that he spends much of his interview talking to me through his parrot.

I am asked to admire the parrot. It is indeed a fine parrot.

There is a feeling high in my stomach. It should be anger but it feels like fear.

I forget the policeman's name or rank but I remember the parrot. The policeman has a popgun, like a child's, into the end of which he puts corks. The parrot moves its head from left to right and shifts its weight from one claw to the other. The inspector raises his gun toward the parrot that must have been six or more feet away. The gun goes off, or does the parrot jump first? The cork shoots past the parrot's perch.

As the parrot flies up it cries, 'Missed. Missed.' and flies back down again.

The inspector of police laughs. A deep laugh as though he'd never seen the parrot do this before. Even though this is a show for my benefit, I am intruding on their double act. I am going to be brief because I hate this man.

I explain about the approach the man made to me to carry goods for him; that this man had claimed that no sniffer dogs would catch me out; that I would never be implicated because I would never have been seen to place the freight - that was the word he had used, 'freight'. There was the hint of a threat if I didn't do it, but it was difficult to be sure.

The policeman is attentive but puzzled.

'So it is not drugs, you think?'

'They want me to take what sounds like a legitimate cargo. A smallish amount of boulders.'

The inspector still looks puzzled.

'Rocks,' I say. I explain that it can't be legitimate because of the nature of the approach. The inspector understands this. He takes the phone number I give him, but he is more intrigued by something else.

'£5,000?' he says. 'That is not the normal amount of money.'

'Too high or too low?'

'And usually they use boats, I think. From Spain.'

I shrug.

'One ignores things like this, the first time.'

'You ignore it or I do?'

'You. They do not want someone who is not interested. They think you need money. And people who have lorries on their own are more...'

'Vulnerable,' I say.

'Vulnerable. You cannot change the routes you use. It is not easy for you to change. You are an easy target. The phone number that they gave you is probably...'

'Untraceable?'

'Untraceable. These modern phones with the cards.' His English seems to be breaking up more rapidly. He doesn't know the phrase we use for pay-as-you-go phones.

He says, 'One can give a false name and address when one registers. I cannot trace the person through the number.' He takes the number anyway. 'But you never know. I've got a tape of the parrot talking.'

'What?'

'Sometimes the parrot does not want to go in its cage at night. It flies around and around the room, up high. Usually in fact.'

The inspector spends some time trying to get an English word from me, we get stuck because I don't know the relevant Spanish.

'Colander,' I say.

'Yes, colander. So I leave the room and the parrot does not know where I am, and I put a colander on my head.' He mimes this, to show me that the handle of the colander went down his back. 'And I walk slowly in to the room and the parrot is terrified and she flies straight into her cage and stands still, wincing. She's afraid and she only looks happy when I shut her cage and I take it off my head again.'

His English had improved. He'd told the story before to the English.

'You don't look like a trucker, Mr Renard.'

The first person to actually say it. I explain about my business going under.

'What did you make?'

'I had a theory. That the money was in mail order and the internet. That there are some things that people want or need, but they are too ashamed to buy in a shop. So they don't shop around for the best price, they are grateful for mail order or the internet to avoid their shame.'

'What goods?' asks the policeman. This is why I always tell my story this way.

'Incontinence pants,' I say. But he doesn't know the English word 'incontinence' and I don't know the Spanish. By the time we sort it out, the moment has gone. It isn't funny any more.

'But not just incontinence pants. All sorts of stuff; long handled scrubbing brushes so that old folk can stand in the shower and scrub their feet. But pants, that's where it started - all sizes - small ones to fit old ladies like little birds; rubber knickers you could fit five people in...'

The inspector smiles, 'So what went wrong?'

'Too many small orders. Old folk are thrifty. They kept washing them and putting them on the line. They'd pass them on to their friends when their husband had died. We tried to move sideways into distribution and import and export, but we could never get the company big enough to make sense of it all. The banks lost interest. In both senses of the word. By the time I was divorced I was left with not one penny. Not one. Just the shirt I had on.'

'Lorries full of rubber pants,' chews the inspector. He and his parrot are the epitome of sanity.

He asks me more questions. He takes an interest in me personally, but he's crap. He will never help me. I have wasted my time. I have registered my story, which may prove useful, but now I want to go.

I remember my news stories: war, cynical pop star, spot picking. Six hours driving left in the day.

DAVID

To put things in perspective we are about 23 days before Ray's death, and 58 days before Chrissie's.

You wouldn't think that to look at me. Legs up on the desk intertwined like two snakes mating. My head thrown back on my chair so that my Adam's apple looks like a pyramid. The thick rectangular frames of my glasses askew on my face to imply carelessness, my pencil thin lips parted asymmetrically to show I'm asleep and drooling.

Between my lips we see some crooked teeth: I draw them like those tank obstacles they used to put on beaches. To complete the image I draw shiny cheeks and outsized clothing to imply youth and low pay.

I had just polished off the Reapham Gazette's banner and was having a little relax before submitting it to the editor. The first item read 'Wilburton Woman in Bingo Win. See page 7.' I amused myself by adding the words 'Picture Exclusive.' The Daily Mail weren't going to get their hands on that baby.

It had taken me twenty minutes of wrestling with the computer to retrieve a story I wrote two years ago about a bingo win of similar import and then another twenty minutes rewriting it. If I could have been bothered to write a new one from scratch it would have taken me a fraction of the time.

I had spent the earlier part of the morning trying to fill a four page 'supplement' celebrating the Reapham annual carnival. I used as many pictures as possible to minimise the text I'd have to write. Cute photos of the nine year old majorettes; a long suffering heavy horse with feral children clambering over it, pulling at its rosettes; and this year's winning float is... see back page.

The Kings Of The Wild Frontier had won best float four years in a row. Their gap toothed smiles, their facial hair down to their waists, the shotguns on their hips. How could they lose? I've always hoped that the judges are fully aware that these people looked like this all year round, and give them the prize for the fun of it. Sadly this is unlikely.

Julio arrived. Julio Barrio is the proprietor of the Reapham Gazette and I tend to see far more of him than I do of the editor. He is an excitable Italian. The word 'excitable' often precedes the word 'Italian', just as 'dashing' precedes 'Major' or 'amok' is preceded by 'run'. No one drinks amok. But I digress. Habitually, as it happens.

My excitable Italian is a caricaturist's dream. He has big bushy eyebrows that curl upwards in a butterfly shape giving him the appearance of a werewolf, but his eyes are round and eager, like a basset hound told it's time for a walk. To top the look, Julio has a swathe of white hair that gets lost in the air somewhere above his head. He's the least groomed Italian I've ever met.

Julio is in his seventies. He always wears neat cream coloured suits. In the 1950s some woman told him he looked sexy in them and he's worn them ever since.

Interestingly, Julio is as short as Matt, but he's more in proportion. It's like David Bowie or Demi Moore, who in real life are very short but look normal in photographs, or conversely William Hague, who in real life is tall. It's the proportions that count, and it affects how they are perceived. So to draw Julio I put him in proportion but put other items in the drawing that loom large around him.

The diminutive Julio was standing in my office demanding what I was going to do about the crop circles. I suggested we ran a story.

Incorrect response.

These crop circles were so exciting that the entire issue should be devoted to it and everything we'd done so far should be trashed.

'But the carnival supplement stays, right?' I asked. I tried my aggrieved stare but in my alarm at the work that was now necessary I looked more like a startled rabbit.

Okay now I'm going to digress to explain a few things about Julio. I'm a frustrating storyteller.

Julio came to the Fens as an Italian prisoner of war. Beet was being farmed because it could be made into explosives and the Italians were brought out by train to work on the fields.

On the first day, the farmer took them off to dig a drainage ditch for one of the fields. There was never a sense that the Italians were a threat - there was no attempt to lock them up for example - but as the farmer took them off to the field he took his shotgun just in case.

He had no means of communicating with them so he stood in front of them and mimed that they should dig a ditch and showed them where. He gave each of them a shovel and left them to it.

An hour later he returned to see how they were getting on. They hadn't dug any further at all. One of them was lying on his stomach howling, a second and third were on their knees praying and sobbing. The fourth was standing, apparently talking to a tree. It seems he'd shat himself.

The farmer was cross with them and started digging himself to show them what he wanted them to do, at which point one of the Italians fell at his feet and seemed to be begging.

The farmer set off back to Reapham and returned with a translator. It turned out the Italians had thought they'd been asked to dig their own graves prior to being shot.

When the truth was explained they cheered up remarkably quickly, and set about digging. Digging round here is not hard; the soil is so soft that East End criminals are in the habit of burying dead bodies in it, that then tend to get ploughed up by the farmers in spring, and ploughed in again at autumn time.

So anyway, legend has it that Julio was the one who shat himself.

The Italians settled in nicely. On a Saturday night they would amble in large groups up and down the High Street, presumably because that's what they did back home. The locals used to hang on their gates and watch them, thus both the locals and the Italians had found something to do. Then Julio had the idea of setting up a cinema for the Italians. This was basically a tent in the grounds of the rectory. Apparently the first film they showed was an old print of Mrs Miniver. Presumably its depiction of English village life was less puzzling for the Italians than it was for us.

Just across the road was a proper cinema from which I believe Julio borrowed the films. The Yanks used to go to that one, and the story was that they were let in free if they parked their army vehicles in the car park. The cinema owner would then send his son out to siphon off some petrol or diesel from each one to sell on the black market.

It was all stored in drums under the stage and was a great little earner until a cleaner was down there one day and lit up a fag.

There was a fair amount of the cinema left after the explosion, but the owner's heart wasn't in rebuilding it so Julio bought it up. This was the first part of his empire.

His other lucrative business at that time was to sell hard core to the Yanks when they built air strips. He would pick it up free, when no one was looking, from bomb sites. He'd then drive through the front gate of the air base with the lorryful, getting it ticked off as having been delivered. He'd drive to the far end of the airfield, out through the gap in the fence, then back round to the front gate again to be signed off as many times as they could get away with it.

The nice thing about Julio was that he does these things as much for the fun as the financial gain. Either way he has ended up with a daunting range of companies, including newspapers, haulage and hotels. He would go into any business if it felt right and appealed to his sense of humour.

To an outsider, the Fens are probably about the countryside. Big sky: keep the horizon flat and low on the page. About the long straight dykes and droves, the plain of fields: diagonal charcoal lines intersecting in flattened diamonds, broken with vertical dashes of identical poplar trees. But it doesn't count for much. We don't riot in the streets; we don't have a famous football team; our countryside isn't as seductive as the counties around us; our industries like haulage and farming aren't considered interesting: in real terms we aren't on the map. It's a shame. To me the Fens are largely about the stories we tell each other: the people and folklore. People like Julio and their antics. It's frustrating for us that we can't get that across.

Julio drove me out to the crop circles. He was arranging photographs and wanted me to interview Matt.

The nearest tall building to the crop circles was Arkwrights, a shop on the edge of the Fens. The joke goes that Reapham is a town where even the cafes shut for lunch. This is, of course, untrue: there is always Arkwrights. It opens at five thirty every morning to do breakfasts for people doing the early shift at the mill or off to work on the fields.

It's very dark inside the shop and jam packed with everything you could imagine from betamax videotapes to dented tins of food in a bewildering array of foreign languages. A particular favourite of mine is the Coronation Souvenir crockery that they stocked in 1952 and still haven't sold. They have at least gone up in value. The trouble is that the shopkeeper re-prices them every few years, upwards, to reflect that fact that they're collectable. He hasn't sold a piece in fifty years.

The sign outside the shop reads, and I'm not making this up, 'Cafe' and then below that it says 'Chiropody' and below that it says 'Agricultural Hire'. It makes you really want to eat there. People say that the woman who owns it has got a dead fowl up her skirt, a sort of low lying lump with legs poking out, that undulate when she becomes agitated. This story is apparently based on no evidence whatever.

We got there to discover the unholy duo of Matt and Matt's father, Matthew, all larking around with ladders on the side of the building.

'We can't get a crop sprayer up in this weather, so we're going to try and take pictures from the top of the building,' said Julio. 'We really need some better pictures of these crop circles before we lose them.' He lowered his voice. 'I've had a bit of a walk round them. Tidying them up, you understand.'

'I don't want to know Julio,' I said.

Julio turned. He was temporarily distracted by something.

'You should see the new wax treatment I've had done,' he said. At first I thought he meant his legs, but he pointed to his car.

I admired his car. A bright red Ferrari. A wizened white haired man and his boy racer. Oddly he was too elderly for it to be sad: it was merely surreal. I couldn't see anything special about the wax treatment but admired it anyway.

We turned back to the project in hand. The ladder was scary-long and, to my eye, very unsafe. Matt got his father to hold the bottom and started up it. At about the fifth rung he came back down and walked towards us.

'I'll need the camera,' he said.

Julio handed over the camera. Matt didn't look well to me.

'You alright?' I asked.

'Oh don't,' he replied.

He pulled up his shirt to reveal the bandage round his waist. It was largely stale red, with concentric rings of weeping yellow.

'What have you done?' I asked.

'I had a fight with a window,' he said.

Julio was restless. 'Go on, before the weather turns,' he said.

Matt started up the ladder again. He called to his Father, 'No matter what you do, Dad, hold on to that ladder.'

'Don't worry lad, I'm holding on.'

Matt was soon halfway up the ladder. He called down, 'You keep holding that ladder, Dad.'

Julio shouted, 'Now remember it's point and click.'

Matt was at the top of the ladder. He took two hands off to fiddle with the camera.

'No,' shouted Julio to the wind, 'Not click and point.'

Matt shouted to his father, 'You hold on now Dad!'

Matt fell off the ladder.

'I'm holding on, lad,' said his father.

Matt was already by his dad's legs.

Matt's father repositioned his feet further apart to get more power into his stance. He was now standing on his son's hand.

'I'm holding on, lad,' he kept saying. 'I'm holding on.'

From where I was standing, I swear I could hear the crunching of bones.

'Oh come on!' I said. 'No one's that thick.' We all rushed forward to help.

MIKE

The three magistrates were behind a raised desk, set against a white blank wall that was unnecessarily tall and wide. They looked dark by contrast.

They were silent and largely still. One of them periodically flicked their eyes up to the clock set above the courtroom door.

The Monkey on a Stick took the stand. It transpired he was called Matt.

'Judging by his hair, he should've been called Gloss,' I muttered to myself.

An usher looked at me over his specs for talking.

Matt had added to his look by wearing an anorak with some paint splattered on it. One hand seemed to be lost inside his coat as if it were broken. With the other hand he kept licking down some of his hair that wasn't standing up in the first place, presumably to show he respected the court.

A drunk from a previous case sat down in the visitors' seating with me. We all waited for the court to get its papers in order.

The duty solicitor walked in. She was eleven and short and harassed and warty and wore a dark trouser suit.

Matt said, 'Hello Carol.'

She replied, 'Hello Matt.' Her smile was genuine. She delivered some papers and left.

The drunk next to me leant my way.

'What are you up for?'

'I have no idea,' I replied.

He nodded. 'That happens a lot,' he said.

The charges were read out to the effect that on the night of whatever, Matt Whatever did wilfully cause criminal damage to the value of less than five thousand pounds.

The court solicitor asked if the defendant was willing to plead.

'Yes your honour.'

'Do you plead guilty or not guilty?'

'Don't know.'

The court became motionless again, except the one magistrate who kept flicking her eyes up to the clock.

'You can't plead "Don't know",' advised the court solicitor. 'Do you plead guilty or not guilty?'

'Dunno.'

'Why don't you know?'

Matt considered this.

'Well the Police issued a description of the person who did it and it does sound a lot like me,' he said. 'So.' He paused. 'You know?'

It was decided that the duty solicitor should take Matt away. There was no clue as to when he would return, and no clue as to why no one pointed out that he was caught red-handed or why they seemed to have dropped firearms charges.

Chrissie appeared and sat down next to me. I explained that she'd missed what little action there was to see; she shrugged and I asked her to have lunch with me. She looked as though I was bothering her by asking at all, but then checked herself and nodded.

We sat by the river.

She looked at her watch and said, 'I'll just have a quick salad.'

I ordered two courses for myself that would obviously take a long while to eat.

Chrissie wore an oversize jacket that was expensive and black; the sleeves came down over her palms and she clutched them. She was asking the world not to take her seriously; like her jacket, she was on loan from somewhere else and might have to go back.

I said, 'Don't you ever want to talk?'

'Not as much as you.'

We both waited to see if she was joking, then I laughed.

'I saw a film at the Arts!' she said brightly.

'And?'

'And a few of the characters died from a broken heart, and a few from poverty. But mostly they died from both.'

She'd been speaking English all her life, but clearly it hadn't been long enough.

'There was a long deathbed scene. But finally the woman concerned came out of hospital,' she said.

'In what sort of vehicle?'

'They didn't make that clear.'

There was a pause.

'You see,' I said, 'if it had been a hearse...'

'Yeah, I did get the joke, Mike.'

'Was the film any good?'

'No. It needed a star to lift it.'

'How do you define a star?' I asked.

For the first time Chrissie gave her answer a lot of thought. 'A star is self sufficient and strong. You know them, but they are holding something back.'

'So Juliette Binoche is a star, but Sally Field is an actress.'

'Correct,' said Chrissie.

I looked away, towards the river.

She said, 'Tell me, what exactly do you see in me?'

'Your energy. Your intelligence. Your sense of fun. Your eyes. Your lips. Your body.'

'My lips?'

'The way they're full. The way they're always held just that little bit apart.'

'That's because I can't breathe,' she said.

'What?'

'My nose has been blocked most of my life. I always have to breathe through my mouth. 24:7.'

'I never knew that.'

She said, 'When we kiss I can't breathe. Did you not know that either?'

I told her some other features I liked about her then launched into a story about my work. Chrissie put on her sunglasses so that I wouldn't see her eyes glaze.

We had sex that afternoon.

'I'm going in. Under your skin. And I'll stay there, like a spore.' Chrissie said this as though singing it to herself.

She put her hair in a topknot before fucking. She climbed on my cock and fucked herself. I would wince at first. Her topknot banged forwards and backwards, lashing her face like a whip. Her arse kept riding. I held her hips and help her forwards and backwards, grinding against me. She looked through the wall beyond. I came and went and she kept riding.

When she finished she looked down on me as if seeing me for the first time.

She climbed off my lap and dripped on the floor.

'I think women use their hands at that stage,' I said.

My pubic hair was soggy, matted with creams and reds and pinks. She must have been bleeding; the colours had mixed and clotted. It looked like Muller Fruit Corner down there.

She sat on the side of the bed with her legs apart. She looked boyish and relaxed; distracted. The bedclothes were darkened, wet between her thighs.

'We have a deal. It's a good deal,' she said.

'We have a deal?' I asked.

'We don't owe each other anything. We don't expect anything. We're a series of deals. If you ask me to do something and I agree, we will do it.'

'How does that differ from a normal relationship?'

'There are no underlying assumptions.'

'What's to stop you hurting me?' I asked.

'How could I hurt you? I agree to turn up to a film, to go halves on a holiday. The worst I could do is betray you on one deal.'

It was my turn to look through the wall.

She lowered her voice and softened it. 'You have everything in life. You are strong, you're confident, you have friends. You can afford to do this one relationship my way,' she said.

'Tell me about Matt. Tell me why someone stormed into my house with a shotgun looking for you.'

Chrissie used the remote to turn on the bedside telly. She flicked through the channels. The thirty or forty channels flashed by so fast.

'They're flashing so fast you could spark off epilepsy,' I said.

Chrissie paused on Jerry Springer or something similar. Americans were sitting in a row facing an audience telling us loudly about their lives. The subtitle came up, 'My wife's boyfriend is a transsexual.'

'How about sex again?' she beamed.

She stood in the middle of the room. Naked, her arms out sideways and her eyes shut.

I circled her silently. I kissed her. Sometimes stooping down to kiss her on the leg. Sometimes lingering softly on her breasts. Sometimes at the nape of her neck. Anywhere. Everywhere. Softly circling. I might trace the tip of my finger slowly round the top of her thigh, or across her lips. She might shiver.

I kissed the nape of her neck. My arms encircled her but only making contact with the tips of my fingers against her nipples. Chrissie's head raised up and turned to the left and then to the right.

'Because it's a first date scene,' she said, 'we know there will be misunderstandings and missed opportunities ahead, but we'll get together in the end. There will be scenes of nudity and occasional strong language. There will be themes of an adult nature.'

'Now,' she continued, 'I want to lie down. I want you to push one arm up over my head and you will kneel with your legs under my arse and your cock in me.'

I did as I was told.

'Now,' she said, 'if I want to fuck you I can move my hips, but that's not the point.'

'It isn't?' I said.

'With one hand, part the lips around my clit and keep those fingers there. Now take your other hand and wet a finger in my mouth. Then slowly, imperceptibly, move your finger against the side of my clit. Barely move it. Barely touch it. Almost in a semicircle. And get yourself comfortable, Mike, we're in for a long ride. Now leave your finger on me and lean forward to kiss me,' she said.

I yelped to convey that this was an awkward position for me. My arm was crooked at such an unnatural angle from my body it looked broken.

'Ow! Cramp!' I cried. 'Cramp! Cramp! Cramp!'

We pulled apart and I sorted myself out. After a break we resumed an almost identical position.

'Keep wanking me as we fuck and seal your lips sealing against mine so that I can't breathe. Even if I struggle, don't stop.'

I did as I was told. My hand moving rhythmically, trapped below my pelvis; my arse thrusting; Chrissie struggling and changing colour.

I pulled away.

Chrissie sprang up, annoyed.

'I'm sorry Chrissie. I can't do that.'

'Why not?'

'For a start I was brought up to be nice to women,' I said.

RAY

There is controversy about arms sales from the UK to another country where they violently squashed an uprising in one of their republics. The British Prime Minister is allegedly a liberal sort, but he is seen smiling, almost sweating, with the excitement of meeting this foreign President who is de facto a murderer.

A well-known footballer more famous for his footwork than his brains was asked by his accountant to make out a cheque to Customs for a diamond bracelet he'd bought abroad for his pop star wife. The cheque was returned because he'd made it out to 'Customs and Exercise.' His accountant asked what he was thinking. 'I was thinking what a bloody expensive gym my wife belongs to.'

A website about a sugar beet is a big hit. Tens of thousands of people log on and watch 'Bertie the Beet' in a farm in Suffolk progress from being a seedling to a 20 inch plant. He will be dug up in October.

I'm going to the British police. If I'm stuck with smuggling, or if I'm caught or beaten up, or who knows what, at least I'll have something to tell the jury. I can't think what else to do. The Spanish police might conveniently forget what I'd said to them.

The English policeman does not have a parrot. This is to his credit. He takes notes from time to time. He records the conversation. He is well dressed, albeit that his tie has a couple of tiny comedy policemen on. He is professional, knowledgeable and courteous. But there's something wrong. Has he had a lifetime not trusting the people he speaks to? He has had to learn to be polite, to pretend to respect people.

'What do you want us to do?' he asks.

'Search my truck and search my house.'

'Why?'

'To show I'm not up to anything,' I say.

'That makes no sense,' says the policeman.

'Then what should I do?'

'Do nothing. We've had this before. I had a trucker come to us and we thought we'd let him play along, do the trafficking, and we'd follow and watch. I went along to my colleagues and I kicked arse down there to make it happen,' he says.

I have a vision of a room full of men like the one in front of me. A room of arseholes. It wouldn't be hard to kick arse in a room full of arseholes.

He had motivated them to think larger than just seizing the one haul. He was the good guy. No doubt they talked about resources: stretched resources, prioritising resources.

'But it just didn't work. We put in a huge amount of resource and then got one minor conviction. They're currently forming a special department to do that sort of stuff, so maybe it'll get done again. You know. Maybe next year.'

'Well I can see I've troubled you,' I say.

DAVID

Now to fess up about my flat.

I rent a place from Julio that is in the middle of nowhere above an empty shop. The building is listed. Apparently, it is a fine example of tedious box-like Fen architecture. It would cost a small fortune to do it up and in either event would be pointless because no one needs a shop on the outskirts of town with no proper road to get to it. Not one of Julio's better investments.

Now, we all understand that a flat, unless ruthlessly controlled, soon becomes full of pizza boxes, Indian takeaway tins, yellowed newspapers, beer bottles and cucumbers that have liquefied in their plastic wrapper.

There's a banana in the middle of the sitting room carpet that has blackened and shrivelled so much that it looks like a turd. Or perhaps it is a turd; I've got some pretty unsavoury friends. I am rightfully ashamed, but I've discovered that the act of being ashamed, in itself, doesn't appear to help clear up the mess. More worrying, I've discovered that attempting to clean just makes matters worse.

For example, I can clear up the kitchen. I can allocate an entire Saturday morning to the task. Well, the bit of Saturday morning between me waking up late and the pubs opening. I get out a black bin sack and pile everything in.

But the trouble is that the bin sack sits in the middle of the kitchen and that's a very useful place for a bin to be. So after a while the sack itself is the problem, because it's so full that if you move it, it'll most likely split and go over the floor. So you have to start a second sack alongside. And because I'm a slow learner the whole thing happens again, except that after this has happened a couple of times I can no longer get to the drawer where I keep the bin sacks and I start using carrier bags instead.

The good news is that this represents an excellent shopping opportunity. I need mops, sprays, bleaches, perhaps even overalls and breathing apparatus. But by the time I've organised myself to do this it's already Monday morning and what with the bin sacks that have multiplied and the fact that I couldn't possibly spend one of my weekday evenings sorting things out, the whole situation deteriorates further.

It does encourage me to spend more time at work rather than go home. This does not mean that I get more work done. Oh no. It means I spend more time on the internet and mucking about sending emails to other slackers.

My friend Sue who works at the dentists across the road has got in the habit of sending an email from work during the first hour of every day and replying to it usually takes me up to my first coffee break of the morning.

A normal email friendship would go something like this. Mild surprise to receive an email from someone new, or if I am initiating the friendship then I write a short email, perhaps asking a practical question to encourage a reply.

Now replies shouldn't be immediate in the early days: you don't want to scare them off or appear to be a Johnny No Mates. On the other hand you don't want to show disinterest. You try to give the very best of yourself. You want to be witnessed in your very best light. It's like going on a date: you tell your best stories, you give the other person plenty of time to breath and respond, and so on.

Sue wasn't like this at all.

Sue is chatty and has a lack of guile. She just talks. Her life tumbles off her lips all day long. But none of this is an overture. This is her total friendship package and you are given it instantly. This would never lead to sex, for example. She would probably be like this with everyone if time allowed but by some whim of fate she has chosen me as the person to whom she would cheerfully talk all day.

Sometimes she will write long garrulous emails, click the button to send them and then walk straight over and continue the conversation in my office, before it's even got as far as my computer. In reply to these emails I can write something short or something long. Or not reply at all, and it always feels right, even if she'd sent three or four. In this relationship, and this one only, I too have a lack of guile. All my middle class graduate sensibilities carefully shaped by a lifetime of insecurities have been blown away. It's very liberating.

On this particular day she had not emailed at all. On a whim, I knuckled down to some work instead.

Crop circles and aliens. I had a number of problems. Newspaper articles, whether in a starchy newspaper or a frivolous one, follow similar formats. For my story to be credible I needed to follow the same format as the others.

For example, if you are quoting direct speech, it will hardly ever appear before the fourth paragraph, but rarely later than the fifth. Conversely the last sentence of a news story is often a direct quote: usually something that is witty or offers a final twist.

So I needed to begin with about three paragraphs outlining the story, which meant I had to form a view on the aliens and relate it. I was already convinced that this was just some people dressing up and having a lark, but if that was the paper's view why devote so many pages to it?

I left the first three paragraphs blank and got on with the

quotes. First person narrative nearly always looks credible and most importantly for me, it looks sameish. If you cut out direct quotes from all over the Times, Independent, the Mirror, the Sun, you will be amazed how similar they are. A few people, such as judges or the insane, have recognisable vernacular but that's about it. This was my secret weapon. I had managed to get some quotes out of Matt while he rested at the foot of the ladder and they would look quite credible provided I didn't print a picture of him alongside them.

I feel quite strongly about this. Take the three of us who were involved in the three murders. If you saw snippets of what Ray, Mike and myself had to say the similarities would be striking. This is not surprising: we are all middle class, university-educated males; we read similar newspapers, we are people who have probably had to write reports or, at university, written essays and we are sane enough to know how to conform to the lexicon of our times. Obviously, as you read our prose at length you would start to see the differences between us, but with any other medium, photography for example, you would see the differences straight away.

It's Blind Date syndrome. The budding dater can sit with Cilla and listen to all the responses she likes, but the suitors have contrived to sound similar (similarly awful). What counts is when the screen goes back and she can see the men.

I had just got through thinking all this, but not doing anything practical about it when Sue walked in.

I've sketched Sue many many times but without telling her, because she's so self-conscious. On the face of it she's not exactly a looker. She's got no neck so I sketch her with her shoulders at the level of her ears. She has a square shaped David Coultard face, and short nondescript hair. A long torso and tragically short legs. Basically, if the Addam's family fielded a rugby team she could be their prop forward.

But everyone was in love with her. It was the way she talked in a constant animated stream: something difficult to convey when I draw her.

Or that was my view of it. The essence of cartooning is that it is a vehicle to exaggerate features that I have already recognised. It relies on good initial perception. If that is wrong then so is my depiction. Cartooning doesn't preform in any way. I don't look at Sue and think 'Oh she's Wilma Flintstone.' It celebrates difference. So anyway Sue came in to see me at about ten to one.

'Have you had lunch?' I asked.

'Oh I can't face lunch,' she said. 'Fucking Rick the Prick has put me off eating for life.' She was picking at my lunch as she said this. 'I was up all bloody night. Arsehole.'

She then set about telling me about her last 24 hours.

The police had raided their house the previous morning, accusing Rick of drug dealing.

'Or it might have been ringing,' said Sue. 'stealing to order and swapping plates.'

'I know what ringing is, Sue.'

Sue then spent the lunch hour telling me how the police had found a bit of rusty bike frame in the back garden and on the strength of it Rick had been taken down the police station for the day. When he got back, Sue spent all night shouting at him and threatening to kill him.

Sue went on at such length that I started typing some work as she talked. She didn't seem to mind, and I didn't feel guilty because she had no intention of leaving Rick so on some level we both knew what she had to say was some sort of irrelevancy.

As if to prove my point, at the stroke of two she looked at her watch, kissed me on the forehead and took herself back to work.

'See you tomorrow, Sue.'

'Okay.'

MIKE

Quirky Greek peasants filter down the hills talking about earwax and politics. Weathered drinkers in the Outer Hebrides open their eyes wide in horror. The whisky has run out.

Reapham is about fifteen miles and forty years from where I live in Cambridge. You wouldn't break a sweat finding as many quaint locals as you'd need to match the opening scenes of films like Captain Corelli or Whisky Galore.

In our surgery alone, there's the old woman who always keeps a chewed up stocking in her mouth, encrusted with soggy food and phlegm. Of late she's taken to wearing bin sacks in the High Street tied, according to fashion, around the waist with some string. Her mother had always urged her to save string; now she knew why. As she walked along she would crap on the pavement. She wouldn't stop and squat; the turd would simply fall out, like a horse. It's not clear what she did before bin sacks came along. Wore dresses probably.

Or there's the man who lodged a complaint that his wife's denture didn't fit, although we had no record of making it.

'It fitted my first wife okay,' he explained.

-There's the three year old who has picked up his parent's upper middle class lexicon, who sits in the corner of the surgery and says things like, 'While it is certainly true that I suck my thumb, I have yet to contract worms as a result.'

With the local scene set, we then meet a few useful characters reacting to some news.

A stocky woman in her twenties wearing a nurse's uniform, is standing in the middle of what is clearly a reception area. In the background there are large posters of teeth and warnings not to eat sugar. The dental nurse is as white as her uniform.

'Matthew Griggson,' she says. 'He died last year in a motorbike accident. He was crossing the road in Wicken and the bike came from nowhere.'

The receptionist sitting behind the desk says, 'You alright, Sue?'

'But Emma, you remember him dying, right?'

'Sure.'

'Well he's now in the waiting room.'

Emma scurries round the desk and peeks into the waiting area. There's an elderly woman wearing a belt on the outside of her jumper to keep her breasts up, and a middle-aged man in garage mechanic overalls.

Emma quickly closes the door again.

'That's him alright.'

They both check the appointment book.

Emma says, 'He's got an appointment.'

Sue scrabbles around and pulls out a patient's notes. It has a large tombstone drawn across the face of it and the letters R.I.P..

I appear.

'What's the problem?' I ask.

'Matthew Griggson's in the waiting room.'

'He's early,' I say.

'No he's dead,' hisses Sue.

'In that case he's late,' I say. 'How do you know he's dead?'

'Because Rick worked with someone whose sister lives in Wicken and he came into work saying how...'

'Let me just stop you there,' I say. 'I've told you before not to mark anything on a patient's notes just on a local rumour.'

'It wasn't a local rumour,' protests Sue.

'And certainly not your daft headstone signs,' I say, 'or the fruitcakes you draw, or the letter 'W' followed by half an 'I', denoting the patient is a half-wit.'

I call Mr Griggson through. Sue walks through to the surgery with us.

I sit with Mr Griggson and check his medical history.

'Are you allergic to anything?'

'Pain...' offers Mr Griggson, '...dentists.'

I raise my eyebrows, I've obviously heard it all before.

Mr Griggson looks sweaty, 'I really hate dentists,' he says.

'That's okay, 'cos I really hate patients.'

The guy won't give up. He's too nervous to spot the mood I'm in.

'I'm a terrible patient,' he says.

'And I'm a terrible dentist,' I reply. I touch him gently on the back of his hand. 'Can we stop this and get on with the treatment?'

'Sure,' he says.

We leave the scene with Sue working on Mr Griggson's notes. She is trying to Tippex out the headstone and R.I.P.: in so doing she's inadvertently making them twice as large, but in arctic white against the brown of the card.

The scene a little later is from the patient's point of view. Sue had got over the dead man coming back to life and was now talking garrulously.

For very nervous patients we can give them an injection in the arm. They stay awake but they become sedated and giggly.

Sue's one of those people who uses TV and celebrity gossip as a point of reference for people she doesn't know. So from the patient's perspective we see Sue in her white uniform at the chair side saying, 'Didn't Kylie Minogue look great in those gold hot pants?' while the patient's eyes slowly close. When they open again she's saying, 'What do you reckon Phil Mitchell's going to do now that Goldie's announced...' His eyes shut again. The comic effect is two fold: it implies that Sue can sedate just by talking, but also that no matter how long the patient stays asleep, when he wakes up Sue will still be talking rubbish. To add to the effect, on the next occasion when the patient comes to, Sue is now talking about the antics of the awful lad she lives with, and then episodically about the brutal punishment and ultimately death that Sue is planning for him.

The patient is well out of it, so I reminisce about this technique. The patients get in such a jolly mood that you could open their abdomen and tap dance on their kidneys and their only response would be to help you keep time by clicking their fingers. We've had patients make us stop work so they can start singing. After their teeth have come out, we've even danced with them around the surgery, with the occasional break for them to spit blood out in the spittoon.

There are a few quirks with the 'hypnotic' drugs however. One is that they induce amnesia - useful if the procedure is painful or you've been dancing them round the room - another is that time and again they give people sexual hallucinations. Oddly enough, unlike the reality, these are often remembered.

We were distracted by the patient. Mr Griggson's hand was coming towards Sue for a grope. I was drilling his tooth and needed both hands. Sue pushed the patient's hand back where it belonged and got on with her suction.

The patient's hand came out again. Sue replaced it. It came out more forcefully this time, trying to slide up her thigh. Sue was wrestling with him now. The patient's mouth was jerking backwards and forwards against the drill. Sue abandoned her suction and employed her entire strength to push this man away.

Water was bubbling up out of his mouth where she was failing to suck it.

I called a halt to the procedure, and brought the dental chair up.

'Come on Mr Griggson. You and I are going to have a dance. Have you ever sang the Toothy Peg Get Better Song?'

Cut again to later in the day. I was visiting a Fen house that was simply not on the map. The locals call it Sanity Row. It is on a common where people had settled temporarily during the last hundred years, some of them gypsies, and their caravans had become more and more permanent. As the years had gone by, they had built a lean-to against the caravan, and then a permanent roof over the top, eventually they had arranged for their generators to be replaced by mains electricity and so on. There was never a day when the caravans finally went and bungalows stood in their place. There was never a day when the council took sufficient interest to lay down the law, or to build a road for them, so the practice has continued into the 21st century. There are no deeds to most of these houses so they are bought and sold cheaply for cash.

Some of the houses now have caravans of their own parked alongside for when the householder wants to get away. Many of the houses have vestigial cart wheels set into the plaster on the outside walls.

So much for the unfilmable back story.

I bounced over the potholes in my four by four and let myself in the back of the house, as is frequently the custom in the older households. I wandered through to the front to find the patient who sat in the dark.

The patient was Chrissie's mother, Beth. She was wheelchair bound and endured guilt-inducing poverty.

'So,' she said, 'you're the man who likes to take my

daughter from behind?'

I didn't miss a beat. 'Indeed,' I said. 'And you are a very scary woman.'

'I've got to amuse myself somehow, stuck here day after day.'

Beth talked a little more about this and that, she sounded very 'old money' but had a terrible coughing wheeze every other sentence.

She pulled her lower denture out and held her lip down with her thumb to show me her gum. It had a mass of four day old mulched bread on it, mixed with what looked the seeds from mustard and cress.

I ostentatiously pulled on some surgical gloves.

There was a home help sitting by the window having a cup of coffee. I hadn't seen her at first so I double took, Cary Grant style. I wish. The television was on in the corner. The local news.

The home help had a broad Fen accent. 'Do you want anything?' she asked.

'More free time and boundless wealth?' I replied.

I explained that I was going to need to trim the denture to make it less sore. I looked for an electricity point for my drill, but there appeared to be only one electricity point in the room. It was round pin and there was a short length of wire leading to a home made adapter and fed the TV.

'Well I've never heard that expression before,' said the home help.

'What expression?' I asked.

'More free time and boundless wealth.'

'It's not an expression,' I replied.

'Yes it is.' She turned to Beth. 'Have you ever heard of that before?'

Beth shook her head. It occurred to me that she was dumbing

down to attract company but I had only visceral evidence for this.

Beth coughed and wheezed for an alarmingly long time then settled again.

'If you've never heard it before, how do you know it's an expression?' I asked and got back to the denture.

Beth became agitated. I had blocked her view of the television.

'We're waiting to see if there's a story about those crop circles,' explained the home help, 'not often something happens in Reapham.'

I moved, and in moving I saw the clock. It stood beside Beth. It was a grandmother clock that was not in good condition: it had wood inlay work that was peeling up at the edges and at some time the mechanism had stopped, because slap bang in the middle of the clock face someone had blu-tacked a second clock. It was a plastic battery operated clock from perhaps the 1970s. Or perhaps the clock had stopped and they couldn't be bothered to wind it up.

'So what does it mean then?' asked the home help.

'What?'

'More free time and boundless wealth.'

My hand hovered over the electricity socket to plug in my drill. Both women tensed at the idea of turning off the television. I set off to the kitchen to see if there was an electricity point there. There was a new washing machine and tumble dryer there.

'Did Chrissie buy you these?' I called. There were shelves of ornaments in the kitchen, many of them broken and re-glued; china cats, ornamental plates, anything that was breakable was broken and the bits were usually not quite put back straight.

'Someone in the house dusts violently,' I said.

I got back to the living room.

'Chrissie's father used to beat me you know.'

I said something neutral.

'Over and over again. I don't know why. It's so long ago, I forget why, or why I put up with it.' She was very matter of fact. 'He was so small you wouldn't think it was possible.'

'One day he fell down. He sort of fainted. He just lay on the floor and he didn't move and I called out to him, but he didn't move. He had diabetes but we didn't know that at the time. So I didn't know what to do. Well what could I do in my chair?'

'Ring for an ambulance?' I suggested.

'So I pushed my chair forward to push him to see if it woke him up.'

'Did it?'

'No. So I took more of a run up with my wheelchair and pushed him hard and sort of ran over the edge of him. Well I felt good. So I did it again.'

I waited, but there was no more.

I changed the subject to another elderly patient of mine that Beth and the home help both knew.

'Oh she died,' said the home help.

'Oh dear,' I said. 'How?'

'She got iller.'

'Ah.'

'She didn't want to eat, so they stopped forcing her,' said the home help.

'Oh dear,' I said. 'That's quite common. It's more common that they wait till you get pneumonia then don't treat you.'

They both nodded.

'There must be thousands of people killed every year like that,' said Beth.

'I saw your mum today,' I said.

Chrissie look sublime. The modern classic Helena Bonham

Carter of Mighty Aphrodite, not the faux-grunge Bonham Carter in Fight Club.

'You know, she still vows to kill my father when she catches up with him,' she said.

'She was more worried about the elderly being killed off today.'

'She writes these long hand-written letters to the chancellor about the pensioners or newsreaders because they said "who" when they should have said "whom." Poor woman.' Chrissie barely seemed to be listening to herself as she talked.

It was early evening. She was wearing a charcoal suit. A Nehru jacket, but trousers with broad flares. She was standing leafing through a fashion magazine. At the other end of the kitchen I was making margaritas. Chrissie undid the buttons of her jacket: she was wearing nothing underneath. She tumbled herself backwards over the arm of the sofa. I could now only see her legs and, beyond that, the magazine.

'You see,' she said, 'women don't understand basques. They think they're wearing them to please men.'

'Aren't they?'

She turned the magazine round so that I could see, then started reading it again.

'A basque should come down low in a V shape and dig in tight. This means that when you're fucked from behind, your G-spot is pushed back hard against the tip of your cock. It makes for terrific orgasms. Or you can get a belt. Pass it low around my waist and pull hard as you fuck. Or you can get your hand and push it hard and low to my stomach or...'

'Chrissie sweetheart?'

'Mmmm?'

I approached with the margaritas.

'We need to talk,' I said.

'Ugh huh?'

51

'Chrissie, here's the thing. Men are brought up to believe that they're bad at sex.'

'Yeah.'

Chrissie balanced her cocktail glass on her bare stomach. I looked nervous. As she talked it tilted alarmingly.

'But it's partly that women are wired up differently from each other and have different tastes in what they want.'

Chrissie agreed again. Her glass gave a jolt. The yellowy liquid slopped up to the side of the glass pulling down the salt from the rim. I lurched forward to save it, then stopped myself.

'And we're taught to feel ashamed of anything extreme we might want to try.'

'You dirty old man,' said Chrissie.

'But when women do the same, they're said to be exploring their sexuality or becoming liberated.'

'We certainly don't want men exploring their sexuality,' said Chrissie. 'You lot are stronger than us; we could get hurt.'

'You have previous sexual experience,' I said. 'You must know all sorts of things that work for you. So what I'm asking is that, like the other day, you simply tell me what you want, and then I'll feel confident providing it. I haven't known you very long, so I need guidance.'

'You barely know me at all,' she said. The drink was now slopping in circles around the glass. Chrissie giggled. She steadied the glass with her stomach muscles, then wobbled it again. She had been teasing me all along.

'So basically I can have anything I like,' she said, 'no more or less.'

'Yes.'

'Ah. I can't possibly agree to that. Women have to be demure, and men have to feel inadequate.'

'This should be the advantage of two confident people dating,' I said.

Chrissie put her magazine and glass down, and stood.

'Slip your hands inside my jacket,' she said. 'Feel my tits gently. Just the tips of them.'

'When we get upstairs, I want you to find a belt for us to use,' she said.

RAY

I have all day to think. Sometimes after a day's driving I wonder what I could have possibly thought about to have filled all that time. But I know what it will have been. I will have been thinking about the past. I will have been re-enacting my life with Jeanie. Or mulling over my life as it is left. But never the future.

During the bankruptcy I was marginalized. Literally, I had to move east. Our county has an affluent corridor that rises up from London. House prices are set by wealthy commuters and businesses keen to locate close to the Home Counties but on the path to the Midlands. I could no longer afford to live there but neither could I face moving further afield to Norfolk. This left me with few options.

I managed to salvage a few thousand pounds and heard about some houses out near Ely, which weren't supposed to be there. They had been built on common land and had no deeds. They could only be bought for cash and because there was a question over them and they were poorly served, they were dirt cheap. They are also very dull and isolated and dank, but I had little choice but to buy one at the time.

I dread going home there. The house is bare apart from a few bits of furniture I took from Jeanie. There is no carpet, just a few rugs and some tatty floorboards. It makes no difference, I have no visitors.

There aren't net curtains in our area, but there should be, to shield everyone from how dull life is. No nets to twitch, nothing to twitch them for. You never meet anyone, you never get to know anyone, a part of the country where life died. People call it Sanity Row, which does at least demonstrate that people in the area understand irony.

I occasionally see a friend, but not often. I used to be a captain of industry, for Christ's sake. I used to get invitations to go to Westminster to some conference or panel or jolly. Politicians used to pretend to listen to me. I used to be dined to death by clients. I used to inflict the same on customers. I used to yearn for a meal that was rustled up on a stove, that didn't come from a menu. Something that wasn't something special from the chef. Because it all tasted the same or smelled the same, because it all came from the same packet. But I was too busy. I was too busy working or making money or going under. I was too busy to make proper friends.

The moment I went belly up, all these people disappeared. It was not unexpected. I never imagined they were anything other than people I knew through work. It is simply that it left a void where all these people used to be.

Once a week, if I am at home, Alan and I go to a pub near where he lives. He's got one decent local that hasn't been repackaged by a brewery to look like every other pub in town. The one decent pub that doesn't smell like a MacDonalds because they insist on providing a quality range of home cooked lunches. Whose home, and what kind of food do they eat there?

I sit at the corner of the bar facing Alan. He is telling me about a problem he is having at work. I'm not listening. I'm thinking how much I know about him and wondering if he is conscious that everyone knows his business.

He is mild and people presume this means he is kind. He met Carolyn at a party. Carolyn. He talked to her gently and took an interest in her life. She used to be an administrator at the local college and then she had children and now she's not quite sure what she wants to do. Within six weeks Alan was stalking her. He wasn't going to kill her, but as she walked the children to school she would emerge from a side street pushing a buggy, and his car would drive past and he would smile.

She thought it was coincidence. Large numbers of people have early morning routines that you can time down to a minute. Theirs coincided at that spot. He would smile, or sometimes there would be a small wave. What she hadn't figured out was that it was not his quickest way to work. He lives in an old town and the streets are all over the place. There is always more than one credible way to get from a to b.

On the days it rained Alan was never seen because those were the days he took his wife, Gabby, to the station. She would spot this was the wrong route. One day he was driving along and for some reason, Gabby was walking along talking to Carolyn. Alan was stuck at the light and he had a never-ending 30 seconds as they appeared at the end of the alley and walked towards him. He shrunk lower and lower into his seat until just his hair was showing over the steering wheel. Gabby looked up and wondered what her idiot husband was doing now.

Alan had few male friends, he just wasn't blokey enough, and being friends with women didn't come naturally unless you had sex in mind, so that left stalking. Perhaps that was it.

There is a lull so I ask him how work is going, and he starts telling me again. I think about my rig and where I left it for the night. I think about Alan and his stalking. Or did that happen so long ago, when my wife could tell me all the gossip. Jeanie is gone and I now know nothing. I start thinking whether we will have another drink, or whether it is reasonable to call it a day, to go home to my silent house on my silent common.

I think of Jeanie, although oddly I can barely remember what she looked like.

We had only been married a year. Property prices were shooting through the roof and we bought a house that we couldn't afford, and in one move we became a couple that resented each other's spending. We resented the life we led even though this was precisely the life we'd chosen. Jeanie seemed to have a hundred close girlfriends. They all seemed to be having children. Now she wanted a baby. She would go on about it day after day.

I would be having a bath. I would bring my head out of the water and she would be there and she would be staring at me, literally staring, and she would tell me of some other person who was pregnant.

I would say, 'But they're ten years older than us.' Or 'We've only just bought the house.' Or 'Our careers aren't off the ground yet.' But she would keep staring at me. I was being stalked by my own wife. I kept thinking that I was in the wrong because everyone else had houses and babies. That's what people do, they have houses and babies. They don't stop and think that they can't afford it or that it will probably be the last straw for what love they had. They don't think that they aren't strong enough as people yet, or that they have too much baggage surely, or even that they're too selfish to have children.

Jeanie stopped taking the pill and we used condoms, just so her body would be right. Just for one day in the future, she said. She was unhappy in her job. She could have a baby and I could worry about making sure we got fed, no matter what I was going through. In the evening when I came home from the job that was killing me, I would be the childcare. That's what men do, or else they must feel guilty and despised.

One evening I was sitting watching television and she just stood in front of me.

She said, 'I want a baby'.

I don't remember cracking or seeing red or any such thing. I just stood up and I pushed her back over the arm of a chair. I pushed her down hard and against the curve of her spine, and it must have hurt.

I kept saying, 'You want a baby? You want a baby?'

I ripped her top up and I pulled at her breasts and I sucked them whole and pulled them with my fist and I could just make out her crying. I just kept on shouting 'You want a baby? You want a baby?'

I pulled up her skirt and I pushed my cock into her.

'Is this what you want?'

She just had her head turned away.

She had huge gashes in her arm.

Her pussy was dry and tight.

I fucked her until I came.

I didn't feel guilty at the time or for many years after. It must have been a sign of how resentful I had become of her at the time. She never mentioned it again, and when many years later I brought it up, she said, or claimed, that she couldn't remember the incident.

Her next period was late and I remember driving home and stopping outside the house and I remember thinking about her being pregnant.

I went inside and she was standing in the kitchen and she talked about this and that, and then she mentioned that her period had started, and it was obvious that it was the only thing she wanted to talk about but she hadn't want to mention it first.

That night she wanted sex again. And she sat on my lap screwing me quite neutrally. But it was unusual. She never wanted to have sex during her period.

She said, 'Don't you want a condom now?'

I said 'No,' also neutrally.

She thought a fraction and then she started grinding and humping with a passion. She was gritting her teeth and her eyes looked so alive, more alive and happy in that instant than I'd seen her for years.

She cried 'I love you' over and over again, even though there was no chance of conceiving at that moment.

It was only a matter of weeks, however, before she was telling me she was pregnant. When she said it I felt the ceilings and walls of our little house closing in on me.

'I thought you'd be pleased,' she said. When she saw the look on my face she looked so wretched.

I wanted to say I was pleased but seconds passed by and I didn't bring myself to say it, and it was already too late.

DAVID

I went completely leftfield and attempted to be good at my job. After all, we had what looked like a proper story.

At the edge of our patch is an Immigration Centre. Various asylum seekers get banged up there and on this particular day they took it upon themselves to break out.

I turned up to the editorial meeting. The editor, Francis, had a face like a twisted plimsoll. It's always like that; he was chronically angry about thirty years ago, and his face kind of set that way. Nowadays the only hint of anger is in his habit of repeatedly telling us basics about journalism he feels we don't understand.

When I draw him I use the eyes and eyebrows of Jack Nicholson when he was the Joker in Batman, but I add a crumpled disappointed mouth. Julio barely deals with him, he's not his sort at all, but I think he came with the paper when he bought it.

Anyway, Francis assumed the angle on our immigrant story was cut and dried.

We had some good shots of the police out and about rounding the immigrants up with helicopters and cars.

'Yes,' he said, 'But news is about people.' This is his Set Comment A. 'What quotes have we got?'

'There's a local shopkeeper,' said one of my colleagues,

'who said, "These people have a nerve. They take our housing, they take our social security, they pilfer stuff from our shop, and they take us for a ride."' He also had quotes from a councillor. '"We don't want these people walking around our villages. We are not a multi-lingual community. Most of these people are not fleeing from torture."'

'Why do we always have to quote the ramblings of that man?' I asked.

'Because,' and here Francis paused wearily in order to deliver Set Comment B, 'news is about conflict. It is about people with interesting views.'

'Okay,' I said, 'One of the asylum seekers claims that he was beaten up by some local lads prior to being arrested. That's local conflict. Let's report that.'

'Is there any corroboratory evidence?' said the editor.

'I could get some,' I said.

'Fine, then run an article. If you're going to accuse our locals of anything though, you must get a high standard of proof. You can't go accusing them of crimes based on hearsay.'

'Sure,' I said.

'Okay,' I said. 'And how about for balance we find some local who says, "Well actually I don't mind the immigrants myself. They seem quite nice, and let's face it, if it wasn't for foreigners who would do all the catering jobs and cleaning jobs in London?"'

There was a sense I'd been on my hobby horse too long.

The editor put on his kindly face. 'Firstly, no one says things like that, secondly it's anodyne, and thirdly...' dramatic pause for Set Comment C, '...we must always fit in with our readers' concerns and interests.'

A colleague mumbled 'Resident Nice About Immigrants Shock!' Everyone tittered at my expense.

'The fact that there are jobs going in London is not an issue for our readers,' said the editor making an ostentatious show of kindness towards me.

Julio appeared from nowhere. That was all I needed.

'If you're finished, can I borrow David?' he said.

The editor nodded.

My reputation as the proprietor's little pet duly confirmed, I left the room.

Julio wanted me to interview Justine about the crop circles. I explained that we now had a bigger story and how I felt about it.

'Look David, if you do a good job on these crop circles then I'll get Francis to bounce the immigrants to the middle pages. Okay?'

The previous day I had drawn a cartoon that depicted Julio as a hedgehog with me as a hedgehog next to him, wearing glasses and looking timid. He's egging me on to cross a motorway with him. Julio is proclaiming, 'Welcome to life in the fast lane!' There is a juggernaut bearing down on us, so in the second frame I am trying to skuttle off. Julio is saying, 'Oh where's your sense of fun?' Very much one of his catch phrases. We leave Julio excitedly getting up on his hind legs to experience the thrill of the oncoming truck.

I looked at Julio and mentally curled myself up into a ball. He was holding my car keys out at me.

Justine Dolly works at the root crop packing factory at Reach. They have a conveyor belt with all the carrots coming down and they have to sort them out and get rid of the rotten ones. They all work on piecework but Justine is one of the best because her head is angled in the right direction. She just has to position her body close to the conveyor belt and she's away.

There are a lot of Justines out at the factory: people who would have little chance of employment elsewhere, while almost the entire male contingent are Polish. They are bussed over from Eastern Europe and put in barracks and paid about £2 an hour plus board and lodging. Julio, who owns the place, gets away with it by calling them students and giving them 'diplomas' in agriculture from 'Cambridge' to take home. There's also a stream of generous gestures; ferrying them all to France for day trips, handing out cheap Champagne with pay packets. He rarely uses the same trick twice, keeping his largesse a source of discussion and surprise. His generosity is a legend in the Fens and in this instance brings the Poles' total pay easily up to the level of a whopping £2.10 an hour.

I popped in the factory as arranged and a scream went up. The women who work there make animal noises when they see a man, a sort of lascivious howling. The Poles join in with the joke because they've got nothing better to do. I try to play along with the joke by pulling a suitably smarmy expression. I remove my glasses in slow motion and swirl my hair like the prim secretary who turns out to be good looking all along.

I found Justine who was finishing her shift.

'You're not going to put this in your newspaper are you?' she asked.

'The crop circles are a big story.'

'I'm not like you city people. You city people always want to be the centre of attention. I just want to be left in peace.'

'I could quote you anonymously,' I said, 'and besides I'm not a city person.'

'And I really don't want my picture in the paper,' she said.

Oooh neither did I. 'Actually,' I replied, 'I was going to take the picture of the investigating PC and leave it at that.'

I explained to Justine that articles like that nearly always have a picture of someone to draw the eye and make it all more human. In this case it would make it more credible. I was going to start my article by saying that 'police are baffled by the crop circles that appeared this week...'

'So,' I said, 'tell me what you saw.'

She shrugged. 'There's not much to tell. We saw spirits and they were singing and moaning and talking in a funny language, and stomping the crops down. It's to do with witches.'

Even I won't digress onto the subject of the worryingly large number of people round here who believe in witches. The Reapham rumour mill was regularly full of tales of witchcraft. I'd done a couple of features on it and kept it light. My favourite was a woman who would talk to people in the pub and then that night would appear to them in their bedrooms. I managed to find three people who testified to that happening to them and ran the story as a feature in the middle of the paper. To not run articles like that would be against the spirit of the area, but it's the devil's own job keeping an air of lampoon out of the prose.

I tried to refocus: I didn't have even one usable quote yet. 'Do you feel the crop circles could have been the work of local lads?'

'Oh no, there's no way it was the work of locals like that.'

Lose the last two words and I had something there I could use.

'Were you scared?' I asked.

'I was terrified, and they were so close.'

That should do for quote two.

I tried to keep her talking but she was getting more wary. By this stage we were outside by the car park.

I sat on the step and looked at Justine. Cars rained down.

'Jesus fucking wept,' were, I believe, my exact words.

Huge pieces of car were falling from the heavens. Bits of bumper, car wing, tyres, exhausts, crashing and thumping on the ground.

We ran back inside the factory.

'What the hell was that?' I shouted.

Half the factory workers had come rushing to the doorway to have a look. Justine and I had trouble getting in.

I stole myself another look. As if on cue two car seats came flying out of the air. One of them went through my car window.

When it seemed to be over we poured outside and looked at the sky.

Nothing.

I got my camera from what was left of the car and took pictures of the debris.

Then more rained down. Entire car engines. Bits of chassis. A stray wiper blade. A car aerial. A bonnet. I clicked furiously with my camera hoping that I might get at least one object while it was still in the air. But this was actually very dangerous and I have never seen a need to be brave.

When there had been a lengthy period without ironmongery falling out of the sky, I went to look at my car. A black leatherette car seat was upturned, piercing the screen. Beads of freshly broken glass covered the front seats, like malevolent hailstones.

Justine appeared behind me.

'Do you want a lift home?' she asked.

'You drive?' I asked.

'Why wouldn't I drive?'

I had visions of Justine horizontal on a some sort of booster seat squinting at the road through the top of the steering wheel.

'Well yes please,' I said, 'But I'm going to try and check this out first. See where all this could have come from and get some photos.'

MIKE

'Do what I say, and nobody gets hurt.'

'Pardon?' I said.

'Of course, I can't kill off my lover,' said Chrissie, 'I'd have to find another one and train him up.'

'So what do you want me to do?' I asked. We were both naked. Chrissie was sitting by my side on the edge of the bed. She was very excited.

'I'm going to lean over the bed and you're going to fuck me from behind,' she said. 'Now listen. It's to do with timing. About a minute or two before I think I'm going to come I need you to slip your hand over my mouth so that I can't breathe. Then when I'm out of breath you take your hand away - you're still fucking and wanking me alright?'

I nodded, trying to match her enthusiasm.

'Then,' she continued, 'I get a few gasps of breath that go straight to my head, then you cover my mouth again. And you repeat the cycle, so as I gasp I've got a lot of tension in me. Now I also want your hand low and hard on my stomach: as you fuck me you should be able to feel your cock moving deep against your palm. That'll then get my g-spot dead centre.'

'And I'm still wanking you?' I asked.

'Yes.'

'I have only two hands Chrissie. Mouth, fundus, clit: that's three hands.'

'Damn,' she said. Her eyes flickered as she thought. 'I know. I'll get a butt plug. I brought one just in case. You grease it and slip it up my arse. It'll help push your cock down.'

I stood up.

'Whoa, Chrissie!' I said.

'What?'

'Chrissie, look. I live in a romantic happy world where you and I are exploring sex for the first time together. Getting to know each other. When we try something sexually, I can't keep wondering whether it's something you did with some other bloke, only better with him. It tarnishes the romance.'

'Well I obviously haven't done it before because otherwise I'd have realised it takes too many hands,' she said.

'Yes Chrissie, but if you wear lingerie, I'd like to think you were wearing it for the first time for me. If we're going to use a sex toy then I'd like to see it come out of a new wrapper. Not just idly get one out of your handbag that looks as though it's been through the wash a few times.'

'Oh fuck off Mike. No seriously, fuck off.'

RAY

A countryside protester hits a government minister. They get in a fight. The protester has a mullet hair do.

A famous model uses sandpaper on her arse every day.

A skull was found, perfectly preserved in peat. It was just behind a man's garden: the man instantly confessed to murdering his wife. When they analysed the skull it turned out to be from the Middle Ages. The odd thing was that for months the man had kept pestering the police with made-up problems, as if he wanted to get caught. He had boiled up his wife's body and put it down the drains.

Mullet, sandpaper, guilty murderer.

I park my truck in Spain. I ring the number I am supposed to.

'Hello?' I don't recognise the voice on the other end. 'Who is that, please?'

I give my name.

'And how are you Ray?'

'I'm fine, thank you.'

'Would you like a day off?'

'Excuse me?'

'See the sights. You are always so hard working. You have a day off.'

'I don't have a day.' I explain my schedule. What I do have

is an overdue assignment of car parts to pick up.

'No problem.'

'No problem?'

'You deserve to stay in a hotel. Just once in a while? You sleep in your cab?'

'Quite often.'

'Stay in a hotel. Get some sleep. Use the sauna, use the gym, have a swim, enjoy the bar, have a meal on us.'

'I get the point.'

'We'll leave some money in your cab but just for the hotel.'

I am supposed to be pleased about the money. If I didn't want money what was in it for me otherwise?

'Great,' I say. 'Shall I leave it unlocked?'

'No.'

I stay in a hotel. It's the best bed I've slept in since I went belly-up, but of course, I don't sleep. I long for a crack in the ceiling to look at, but the room is flawless and white. The air conditioning is noisy somewhere in the walls, somewhere in the ceiling, somewhere in the next room, pleasingly noisy; something to listen to. It turns off and in another twenty minutes there's a click and it starts again. This is my night. My own life is more distant every day. I was married once, I owned a company once, people respected me, people talked to me, but I forget the details, I forget why I am so angry. I pass in and out of sleep without knowing. I have no way of knowing. I have no one to check in with.

I remember the first day I met Jeanie.

I said to her, 'I love you.'

She said, 'Don't tell me you love me. Show me you love me.' She was an editor. She thought she was being funny. She was being stupid. In relationships, all decent people talk more than they 'do'.

'I love you,' I said again.

She had been arguing something improbable at a dinner party. She was gleeful at the degree to which she was arguing the impossible, putting men down.

I said, 'I want a date with you tomorrow. And the next day. And the next day.'

I had chosen her.

She stopped in her tracks. This was the most delightful thing she had ever heard.

'You're on!' she said.

The strong woman chose a strong man.

I had ordered a plastics moulder the size of a hanger but twice as tall. When built it would dominate the skyline of the town. It was coming from Canada and would blow the competition away. The cost of raw plastic was sky high but the cost of recycled plastic was low, because so few people could use it in their products. This was the machine to do it. My costs would be a fraction of my competitors. I would be able to make most of my own products rather than contract out, but also I'd be able to recycle plastic for the general market.

I was hiring staff as fast as I could. I would stand in the doorway of the factory and usher the girls in myself. They would know I had a friendly hands-on approach. Meek local girls who had dressed up to be interviewed, looking at me to make them flower. Beaming at me. Thanking me for their job offers.

It's morning. I walk back to my truck in the morning and there's no one in evidence, but I'm sure someone's there watching my movements. But there are no cars, no passers-by, no windows overlooking me; just the smell of early morning in a hot country. Of heat to come.

It's another morning in my truck. I have an English

newspaper which I read in a lay-by.

An international terrorist is convicted and banged away for a few years. Wish washy liberals are moaning that there was no clear evidence against him.

A minor film star is deeply in love with a major film star. So in love that they can't agree in the pre-nup as to whether she should get three million a year for every year spent with him or one million, when they split up one day.

A busy city broker buys a dream house in London. He sets off every morning leaving notes for the builders and decorators. He agonises about the colour of the masonry paint for the Georgian facade. Eventually he chooses something off-white and leaves the colour guide with a post-it note on it to indicate his choice. When he comes home, his house is fluorescent pink: the colour of the post-it note. The decorators were annoyed with the home-owner because it took then half the morning getting that shade of paint mixed right.

Terrorist, pre-nup, pink house. This is my only laugh today. I wonder that the human stories take more explanation than the others.

I fill up my truck with 53p diesel. 53p Spain, 54p France, 83p Britain. I flick around radio stations. I can't find an English language station. I listen to a French station for a while then turn the radio off.

I am probably being followed by a car. It's hard to tell, sometimes there are drivers who tuck in, who drive in your wake, but this is the wrong sort of car. I've got a hunch it's a hired car but I can't be sure. It could be the police, but why would they follow quite so closely? What is wrong with me that I don't care? Perhaps it is because I have to drive hour after hour. I can't just keep thinking, *there's a car behind me, there's a car behind me.* I've got to have other thoughts. Of course, my brain will think of something else, that's natural.

We were struggling with massive debts and Jeanie was at home all day and I was working seven days a week. There was a recession on: property prices had collapsed and we figured - well *I* figured - this was our chance to change premises and expand. Everything was cheap. It was time to take that chance. But it was the wrong part of the business cycle. We were down to our last few pennies. The bank's last few pennies. I was doing everything myself to save money. I was using the two days every weekend to build and refurbish the new offices; I was doing the plumbing, I was laying the wiring myself, I was painting the walls. But I was doing it at the wrong part of the cycle.

We had young children. They would wake four or five times a night. Jean would just sleep. It wasn't her fault she slept heavily. So I would pad around the same bit of carpet with a child on my hip, and spend the daytime eating paracetamol.

I was everything to Jeanie. I was the plumber, the family accountant, the childcare, the lover, the best friend. And Jeanie was many of these things too. We were fully integrated.

I knew every fibre of her. I knew what she would say, what she would think, and every one of her habits. I knew that her remedy for dry hands was bacon fat. I knew her one and only joke was 'Doctor, doctor, in the mornings I keep thinking I'm Donald Duck and in the afternoons I keep thinking I'm Minnie Mouse.' 'Ah,' replies the doctor, 'you keep getting Disney spells.'

I knew she disapproved of cardigans because old folk have trouble pulling clothes over their heads, so we'll be destined to wear them when we're old so why start now. I knew she always got uptight when there were signs at supermarket tills saying 'ten items or less,' when the word they were plainly looking for was 'fewer.' Apparently.

I knew her stock story about how we first met. 'It was at a dinner party where we were all singletons and I put myself up for auction to whoever would offer the most grandiose date.'

On Saturday mornings she would read the Weekend Guardian at the kitchen table. Zeitgeist, PJ Stone, Lost Consonants; in that order. Then she'd go to the back; Dulcie Domum, Questionnaire, Joke. Every week.

There was nothing she could do that would surprise me and I loved it, I genuinely loved it, but I knew that if we were going down together, if our lives were falling out of the sky, she would never turn round and say 'Oh surprise! I had a parachute all along. We're saved.' We would just plummet. Tied together, plummeting.

The phone rang and the bank told me that was it. We'll not honour another cheque. I was taking the piss, apparently. I was only working 24 hours a day, seven days a week. When were they going to see a return? Not one more penny. But we had to eat and live and we had to keep going with the premises. I told them that I was only weeks away from it all turning around. The new plastic moulder was due. It was the point of the loans after all. Why couldn't they wait?

I came home one day and I walked up to the front door of our heavily mortgaged house and I could hear children screaming in there and I could hear Jean screaming and I could hear it was about nothing; it was about eating or about a child getting into a bath or not getting out of the bath, and my hand hovered over the door handle. I felt guilty and such a failure; such a failure for not bringing home the bacon or for wanting to hover there, not wanting to go into the house, not wanting to go in to see the people I chose to live with; my life I chose to live.

I walked in the house and Jean said 'See what you can do with them.' She said it nicely, and in fairness the children looked quite pleased to see me. They both looked at me from the bath and the whingeing subsided. And I would read to them and I was still hungry, and I was trying to be a good person; the father I knew I should be.

The plastics moulder I had ordered was behind in its delivery. Months behind. We were keeping staff for whom we had no use. The price of raw plastic was spinning badly in the wrong direction. The crude oil price had tumbled and suddenly my recycled plastic was no bargain at all. But I would have to service the debt on the machine.

I spent evening after evening looking at the contract I had with the Canadian manufacturers. There was no way out. I was stuffed and I knew it. The bank knew it.

I went downstairs and I was tired and I slumped in a chair and Jean looked irked with me. She would sometimes tell me off because she'd had a boring day. She looked forward to me coming home. Then she'd complain because I had nothing interesting to say.

I sat and opened the mail and it was a gas bill for £312. I remember it: £312. We owed over two million by that stage but I was worried by £312.

She sits at home. She keeps the house like a furnace. She moans that I'm not around and when I am around she sees that as her cue to go off duty. I work. She runs up bills. Although I tell her all the facts, although she can see everything for what it is, she just runs up bills and we can't pay £312.

And she's fat.

I'm not even being thrown a bone here. She was so pretty when we met and now we haven't even got that. She's lazy and she's fat. She's put on a couple of stone. It all went on her stomach and it looks like crepe paper and it sags down between us in bed as though it's not part of her at all, and her face looks bloated. She looks ill with it.

Jesus, when did we get so ordinary? When did we become

people who fell out about menial crap like money or looks or childcare. I thought we were special. Or maybe we were always like this.

I think the worst thing was how indifferent she had become. She didn't see how pale my face was, she didn't see how I worried, she didn't see how I was giving everything. I was dying in front of her and she was asking about getting a better kitchen. The £312 bill, and the babies waking us up at night and Jean being overweight; these might all be temporary, but the indifference, the fact we weren't a team, that was for keeps.

If I'd struggled on my own and made my money over five or ten years and then I'd met Jeanie it would have been so much easier. She'd have loved the luxury. The sports cars, the frivolity of being wealthy and I wouldn't have been resentful: everything would have been sweet. The same people ending up in the same place, but because we'd taken the menial route, and taken it because we had been in love, we were fucked.

The next morning was Sunday morning and the deal was that we took it in turns to get up for the children so that one Sunday in two we each had a lie-in. I took the kids out in the buggy and pushed them across the common, and the wind was hard and cold, and we were going where? Nowhere. A drummed up errand to buy some croissants and a paper for breakfast.

There was toyshop near the French deli; the kids liked to look in the window. It was the highlight of the trip for them. I liked to tell them about the toys I had when I was a kid. They were never interested, but I wanted them to know.

When I got home I woke up Jean because I wanted to explain all the things that I'd been thinking, but when she woke up she looked so far away.

So I told her about my hand hovering at the door the night before. I kept it at that, and that did as much harm as good, because I let slip that I was resentful of them all. She listened and she agreed. She understood. She'd change. But even having to explain the smallest thing chipped away at us, or the having to admit to myself, yes, I do mind that she put on two stone. I'm not supposed to mind, but I do mind.

The car behind has gone now. I have forgotten even what the other car looked like. There is another car there now. But of course there is another car there. This is a road. There will always be other cars.

War, topless starlet, suicidal squaddie. What was it I had been thinking? I've forgotten what else I was thinking and it worries me.

DAVID

It had been a good day. There had been a stabbing at the local chip shop.

A disgruntled employee had come at the manageress with a knife who then retaliated with a ladle of chip fat. It was a story that should please the editor. Local people in conflict.

I wandered in there for a kebab to eat at work and to my joy the story had dropped in my lap and virtually wrote itself. The lad threatened to return when he got out of hospital, so hopefully that will be in time for next week's deadline. It wasn't clear how much of the skin on his face the lad had lost; perhaps there'd even be a story there about facial reconstruction.

I was getting a kebab because the dirty kitchen lark was so beyond control that I was forced to eat my meals at work. I figured the office cleaners could keep the problem under control.

My flat had developed an acrid musk that had taken to waking me in the small hours hissing my name. I presumed the smell emanated from the kitchen, although I couldn't be sure, so I went in there, or attempted to.

In the kitchen I discovered one of my longest standing problems had taken on a new dimension. After cooking I had always been a great believer in that old slacker's standby 'putting things in to soak' because, as we all know, pans end up cleaner if you put them up to their handles in slimy water for three months.

So the sink was full of pans and crockery and crap and, of course, the tap was dripping a little from a faulty washer which helped to keep the primordial soup nicely topped up, complete with dead flies and fetid dish clothes.

There are some pot plants on the windowsill beyond which I've never watered since the first week I bought them when, obviously, I watered them four times a day; but the more sharp-witted plants had had the presence of mind to send tendrils out to the primordial soup and seem to be thriving on it. Since I last looked, these plants had put on a growth spurt so that they now occluded the window, blocking out all natural light. In fact they had gone well beyond the height of the window and were curving back in to the room and glaring at me malevolently.

To disturb the plant at all would be to invite immediate personal danger because up on the ceiling there were thirty or forty brownish insects buzzing in a holding pattern. But at least eight times as many were crawling in and out of the plant top.

I don't like insects. I went off to find some fly spray but soon remembered that it was in the cupboard under the sink and that was beyond reach because of the bin sacks. I returned to the kitchen with the good intention of getting to that spray.

But when I got as far as the doorway I realised that everything stopped. That is to say that there was definite movement in at least two areas of the bin sacked floor but the moment I was present, whatever these things were, had frozen. As did I.

I got some work clothes and my keys and I fled.

Sue came in to the office as I was attacking the kebab. She was pleased with herself.

'I bought a car,' she said, 'I mean it's only a cheap old thing.

One of the girls at work was selling it.'

She stood by the doorway for me to follow and have a look. It was a white Polo. It really had had one careful lady owner. I thought of my car still stuck, windowless, where someone had towed it to my place but I still hadn't got it sorted out with a new windscreen.

'That's terrific,' I said, 'are you taking me for a spin?'

'Oh I can't drive,' she said. 'In fact I thought perhaps...'

Please don't ask me to teach you to drive. Please don't ask me to teach you to drive. Sue continued, 'You might be able to teach me the Highway Code and stuff.'

'Sure.'

'But don't tell Ricky,' she said.

'Why not?'

'I want it to be a surprise, when I passed my test and everything.'

We went back in so that I could finish my kebab and I asked Sue what she thought about the flying car parts.

'Presumably people were standing on the roof of the factory throwing them off,' she said.

'Okay. But why? I looked long and hard at the factory and walked round the back and the only explanation would be that someone was throwing stuff off the roof and it would take a hell of a lot of effort just for the fun of it.'

'Ask the Poles.'

'I couldn't find any English speakers.'

'Who owns that factory?'

'Julio,' I said, 'James Palmos might have an interest in it.'

James Palmos owned the half of Reapham that, by some oversight, Julio hadn't bought up in the sixties. He had a dodgier reputation that Julio. People assumed he was involved in some sort of organised crime, but nothing anyone could substantiate. Unless it got to court one day, it was never going to appear in the press, but when it did, we'd have a Robert Maxwell on our hands and the stories that had previously circulated would prove to be the tip of the iceberg.

Sue was rueful.

'James once helped me,' she said. 'Ricky used to work at a garage he owned, but Rick had been joy-riding in the customers' cars and he got the sack. I pleaded with James for about an hour and got Rick his job back, then when I told Rick he just started hitting me. It was unbelievable. He just resented... I don't know really.'

I waited about ten seconds then brought up the chip shop incident. She knew about the lad involved and gave me a few details about him that were useful.

I asked her if she fancied a drink that evening.

'No I couldn't do that,' she said. 'What with me living with Rick and everything. You know.'

I spent the afternoon down at the Immigrant Reception Centre. I'd had an idea about how to tackle the asylum seekers story. Somewhere in that immigration centre I should be able to find myself an orphan or a torture victim. Perhaps a woman who had been raped and had to watch as her husband was shot. Preferably an orphan though. News is about people. The readers will see the orphan as a human being. I was going to make it personal.

Bizarrely, the centre had no apparent telephone number so I'd been forced to go down there in person to look for my orphan or torture victim.

There was a policeman on the gate. 'Have you got an appointment?' he asked.

'I couldn't find the telephone number to ring to make one,' I replied.

'I'm sorry sir, but I can't let you in without an appointment.'

'I simply wanted to interview a few immigrants about the recent breakout. Apparently at least one of them was assaulted.'

This was the wrong thing to say.

'I'm sorry but you can't...' he appeared to stop himself. '...do that sort of thing without first getting permission.'

'Well can you get someone to the gate for me to ask permission?'

'Who did you say you were?'

'There's no need to be suspicious of me mate.'

'Can you tell me who you are please, Sir?'

I gave my name and showed my press card. He had a walkie-talkie with him. He moved to one side. He was still the other side of the iron gates so it wasn't hard for him to stray beyond hearing range. He could have been talking to his mother for all I knew.

Eventually an official came out but he claimed that he wasn't authorised to let me in.

'Then why did you come out to talk to me?' I asked.

'We use a regional press office to deal with issues like this.' I swear he almost said '...to deal with people like you.' I became very conscious of what a shambles I must have seemed standing there in my crumpled clothes. It was a dispiriting day.

MIKE

Lisa and I walked together to the restaurant. 'So what are we doing?' I asked.

'Thanks for coming with me,' said Lisa. 'She linked her arm through mine. It's just a meal. I couldn't get out of it. They're nice people but, you know, a bit dead.'

We got to the restaurant: a noodle bar. I remarked at the number of noodle bars that had sprung up to replace the sushi bars that had sprung up and gone under the year before.

We sat at long over lit tables. There was an open kitchen running the length of the restaurant. Yards of stainless steel surface shining at us, so intensely bright it lightened the sides of our faces. There was music playing. Woody Allen style clarinet. There were big windows looking onto the street. Pedestrians were hurrying by. It was now raining and they were huddling and hastening.

I took up conversation with a man to my left who had spent the last eight years of his life researching the wing movements of bees while flying.

'They pay you to do that?' I asked. 'I'm sorry. That was rude.'

There was movement by the door of the restaurant. A well-dressed man in his late forties was taking off his coat and shaking an umbrella. He was talking to the owner. He looked over at us a few times and it was obvious that he was going to join us.

Chrissie came and stood by the table.

'I didn't know we were expecting you tonight,' I said.

I looked to Lisa by way of a question. She raised an eyebrow and shook her head.

Chrissie was wearing a dress. It was strapless and dark purple; it hung tight over her angular frame. Something untamed had escaped from a catwalk.

Chrissie came round the table and kissed me on the cheek and did the same to Lisa.

'I'll come and sit next to you,' I said.

I got a stut from Lisa which I ignored. Bee man didn't seem very concerned where I sat.

'I'd better sit with Adam,' said Chrissie.

Adam came over and introduced himself. He spoke slowly. He was assured and monied. My look betrayed the fact I hated him.

'I'm Mike, I'm one of Chrissie's friends,' I said.

He smiled. His teeth were perfect.

'So Adam, what do you do for a living?'

'What a dull question Mike,' said Chrissie.

'I'm a theatre promoter.'

'And what sort of theatre do you promote?' I asked.

'Ballet and opera mostly.' Adam appraised me a second then added, 'I have done some rock tours though.'

'Any groups we've heard of?' asked Lisa.

I smiled. Good one Lisa.

'Radiohead. Aimee Mann. I try to only promote people I believe in. It makes my job easier and so much more pleasurable.'

I smiled at him, lips together. Bastard, wanker, tosspot, git.

'And what do you do?' he asked me.

I pretended not to hear him. I cupped my hand to my ear as if I'd like to hear what he said but somehow couldn't. I then turned myself to renew my profound interest in bee flight.

The bee man was devouring his noodles by the forkful but they were falling out of his mouth again. There was an extractor fan in the kitchen that was louder than I remembered. My face felt clammy.

Chrissie got up to have a pee. The toilets were upstairs so I announced that I ought to relieve myself as well.

I stood outside the women's toilets in a corridor barely a foot wide. A couple of women squeezed past me and it was an eternity before Chrissie appeared.

'Hiya,' she said.

'So who is he?'

'Who?'

'You know full well who.'

'You mean Adam? Oh, you know.'

'No I don't know.'

'Are you going to let me past?' she said.

I heard myself say, 'What does he mean to you?'

'Please let me past.'

'What does he mean to you?'

She said, 'Oh the normal things a husband means to someone. Why?'

DAVID

None of the nationals picked up our story about the crop circles, nor for that matter the story about the chip shop fight. Not too surprising, of course, but I had been getting a rash of rejection slips all week and wasn't feeling too good about myself. I had been sending cartoons off to newspapers and magazines and they'd been coming back again. I started wondering if I should start a collection of my journalism and try to work my way up through to the nationals, but unless they were suddenly going to start taking an interest in stories about rural primary schools and the ongoing debate about the exact positioning of memorial park benches in the town centre, my portfolio wasn't going to quite hit the spot. I'm 23. I can't be in a rut at 23, can I?

I took some tablets. I had a hangover that just wouldn't shift. With my flat the way it was, it was getting very easy to spend the evenings in the pub rather than go home. I decided to spruce myself up a bit. I hunted for my toothpaste which was somewhere in the rubble of my office. If I could just learn to put stuff in a draw it would save hours of my life. The toothpaste was clogged where I'd left the cap off. I unraveled a paperclip and tried to break through the clogged up section of the toothpaste.

I decided to cut through the other end of the tube with some scissors and get the paste out that way but I couldn't find the scissors anywhere. I gave up on brushing my teeth and picked at them with a fingernail instead. I gathered a lot of crud under my nails but I wasn't sure what to do with it, so I ate it.

I spent half an hour gazing into space. Then spotted a cup that had fallen behind the desk.

Some months ago it must have had some dregs of tea or coffee in but now it had grown shoots of grass-like fungus in shades of green and blue that were previously unknown to science. They reached up five or six centimetres beyond the rim. I hunted around for a cigarette lighter and set fire to it. It was tough at first but when it finally went up, the flames were reds and purples and the smoke was so thick you could cast spells in it.

The alarms went off.

I put a pile of papers over the cup and tried to act naturally.

Francis put his head round the door.

'What the hell's gone on in here?' he asked.

'I had a slight accident,' I replied. By then my eyes were streaming with all the fumes.

Smoke was still seeping from the mug and creeping laterally along the desk.

'You had an accident with a mug?' asked the editor.

'Mmmm,' I said.

'Can't you open a window or something?'

'No,' I replied. There was too much rubbish in the way of the window catches.

The alarm stopped so I threw a look at Francis implying I was somehow vindicated.

'Hey look, while I've got you,' I said, 'I need some funds for a story.'

'Go on,' he said.

'I've found an orphan at the immigration centre. He lost his parents in war.' I was lying. 'I thought it would make a nice human-interest piece about the immigrants who live among us. But I might need a translator to get his story.'

'Can't any of his pals translate?'

'The authorities won't help me find a suitable person so I'd need to take one in with me.'

'I'll think about it,' he said.

'Does that mean yes or no?'

'It means I'll think about it. I doubt the orphan's going anywhere in a hurry. You've got other stories to work on. It's only worth investing in if we're going to get several articles out of it.'

'I could write several articles.'

'He's a child. How much is he going to have to say?'

'That's a no then.'

'Find yourself an orphan who speaks English. And clean this bloody office up.'

'There's another angle I could go for.'

'Yeah?'

'The Immigration Centre wouldn't let me talk to the person who claims he was assaulted.'

'Mmmm. Have you ever read a story like that in a local newspaper. Ever? Anywhere? In any kind of newspaper at all?'

'No,' I replied.

'Then it's not just me who feels that is a poor idea for a story.'

'No,' I replied.

'I'll give you three column inches for it.'

'Thank you.'

'Five if you make it interesting.'

'Thank you.'

When the smoke cleared in my office I cheered myself up by doing a cartoon about the Poles. Julio owned a pub in town and he had a bright idea to lay on a coach that took the Polish carrot sorters from their barracks to his pub once a week. Once a week the coach took about fifty of them in for a good drink up and then returned them at closing time. This system worked wonderfully well week after week. The publican and bar staff would stand to attention as they heard the coach pull up in the car park and then a cirrhotic number of vodkas later the pub would be up several hundred quid.

The last couple of weeks had been different however. The coach pulled up, but nothing happened. The bar staff waited and waited. But it turned out the Poles had discovered a better pub up the road: the vodka was cheaper and the women more plentiful. So they were disembarking from the coach and then sinking down below the level of the pub windows in a steady stream and making their way up the road. At ten past eleven they returned, again sinking out of sight as they passed the windows, and were to be seen waiting cheerfully on the coach to be returned to the Fen.

Julio was not impressed. The following week the Poles piled off the coach and then, as before, crept in single file along the side of the pub, ducking down at each window. When the first of them rounded the final corner of the pub they came across Julio standing in the way. He didn't say a word. He didn't need to, he was holding a meat cleaver. The line of Poles piled up in silent confusion.

It made a great cartoon. The scene was lit by the light over the pub sign and I showed the Poles forming a concertina shape between the pub door and the angry Italian. My caption was, 'One way or another the Poles were going to spend the evening cut.'

I got back to sketching. I sketched Susan's Rick. I tried to bring out what she must see in him. I tried to imagine them having sex or sitting watching Brookside or whatever it is they did.

I drew them having sex on the sofa. Sue with a copy of

Cosmo open in her hand, 'Forty Mind Blowing Sex Tips'. Rick rutting away with a speech bubble saying, 'Real men don't hang about Sue, they just stick it in.'

Susan was in my office standing right behind me. She went red. I went green. The air went blue. It was a Technicolor moment.

She stopped swearing eventually.

'If you're going to sneak up on me, Susan.'

'Yeah. Yeah. I'm sorry,' she said. She was walking backwards and out of the office plainly in shock at what she'd seen.

RAY

World leaders meet; they spend their time in Hawaiian shirts and on the front of newspapers. As a result of the summit, books imported over the internet will not be subject to extra taxes. This is the only outcome I find.

A famous author, the son of another famous author, has his teeth done again. It was viciously expensive.

There is a council in London which has so many fast food restaurants that the sewers get silted up with fat. Twice a year they send men and machines down to clear out the tons of fat and, literally, the crap. Despite containing known toxins, this is then sold and put into animal feed.

I have no trouble remembering my news items today. I take this as a good sign.

I pull the rig over to the side of the road. I don't remember deciding to do that. I want to find whatever's hidden in my truck. I just want to look. I get out of the cab. I stand back from it. I stare at it without a clear thought at all.

The freight itself is rocks. Boulders that are surprisingly light. But more amazing, they've been boxed up. They look manufactured rather than quarried. I retrieve one. I lug it to the side of the road. I try to break it open. I lift a bolder and pound it against the side of the road. Barely a fraction chips. I try again, but still it doesn't crack. This is madness. This is all madness. If it was just this freight then they wouldn't have approached me in such a clandestine way. There has to be something else.

I climb up the outside of the cab. I stand on top. I don't like heights so I stick to the middle. I'm looking for some sort of modification to the truck; some riveting or welding or new paint. But no matter how hard I look, there's nothing like that.

I climb down again. I look for breaks in the seals. Sometimes they are cut and superglued again. Nothing. The engine housing? The fuel tank? I know that what I'm looking for must be in front of my eyes but I can't see it. There's hardly going to be a big box marked 'Contraband', but on some level that's what I was expecting to see.

I look up and down the road. I feel they know I am doing this. It's one of those long straight French roads that has a heat haze and no traffic. No traffic today. No one following. Where are all the vehicles that should be on the road? This is a conspiracy. This is Cognac country, or is it Armagnac country? It's flat and empty.

I can't seem to get back in my cab. I don't want to get back in. I'm middle-aged. Middle-aged. Middle weight. Punching above my weight. Lost. Out of my depth. Friendless. I am ripping out pieces from the cab. I am looking at the seating, in the storage lockers. I am pulling at the panelling. I have cut myself. Perhaps on the metal under the seat, or it might have been earlier. There is crimson on the seats. Splashes now. Lines of my blood. They must have been there before. I'll be able to drive - it's just the side of my palm. I look for the first aid kit. I have something I can do. I am sitting by the road and I can't open the first aid kit. There is blood dripping on the kit and smearing as I try to open the cellophane. Cellophane that's difficult to open in an emergency. There is a bandage. Lots of rolls of bandages, but little else. There is a packet of plasters. As fast as I push the bandage against the cut, it bleeds again. It won't stop bleeding long enough to put the plaster on. I am driving. When did I start driving again? I've been driving a long time. My finger aches but not my hand. It's seeping red. I will need more plasters. Did I leave the first aid kit by the side of the road? Yes I did. Perhaps I will find a station to stop at. I shouldn't drive if I feel faint like this, but what choice do I have?

DAVID

I took myself along to see Sue to apologise.

Sue lives in Sanity Row in one of the very few houses that isn't a bungalow. Not far from Ray in fact. Presumably after his 'bankruptcy' he quietly had a few thousand and bought the house outright. The houses round there have no deeds so are dirt cheap.

I found Sue's. It was a plain box of a house in white brick. It had uPVC windows with white plastic latticing on.

I knocked on the door and Sue answered it.

'Yeah?' she asked.

'Can I come in?'

I'd never been in her house before. It was immaculate and in appalling taste. The first thing that caught my eye were three framed views of the countryside, each about six inches wide. They were spaced equidistantly along a broad plain wall. There must have been six foot between each picture, each in a sprayed gold wooden frame; each print little better than a photocopy.

There was the china pierrot bending forward holding an ashtray: proffering it to whomever was on the sofa.

But my personal favourite was a plastic statue in the style of Michelangelo's David, holding up a parasol. About fifty nylon threads ran from the rim of the parasol down to the base. The statue had a plug. When plugged in, David lit up from inside and water was pumped from the base up into the parasol. The water then ran down the nylon threads in a constant raining motion.

And then there was Rick.

I didn't spot him instantly, blinded as I was by the decor. He greeted me, but Sue said nothing. She was standing with one leg on each corner like a lineswoman at Wimbledon. She shifted her weight from one side to the other as though angry or nervous.

'Did you want something ?' she asked.

Rick rose out of his chair. He was taller than I remembered and more elegant.

He was elegant.

'Can I get you something?' he asked. 'You're the reporter man aren't you? Would you like a beer?'

'That would be lovely,' I replied. He went through to the kitchen.

I tried to remember when I'd last met him or even if I'd met him at all. He rings cars, he beats up Sue, he might well have a floozy. He was charming.

He returned with a can of McEwans. He was sinuous. I was not sure how I would caricature him at all. He was a good looking lad largely through symmetry and a lack of flaw. But he had no defining features; no pronounced cheekbones or smouldering eyes. I had so little to go on. He was the nice guy down the pub, the reliable guy at work. Choose any topic of conversation and he'd join in and make you feel good about yourself.

'Actually I was hoping for a word with Sue,' I said.

'Oh. Fine,' said Rick. 'I'll make myself scarce. I need to go out anyway.' He took his car keys from the mantelpiece next to the purple candle in the shape of two lovers intertwined.

Sue suggested we went into the kitchen. When we got there

she didn't sit.

'I just wanted to say I'm sorry,' I said.

'No problem,' she replied.

Silence.

I thought of the cartoon in question. The Herman Munster with her legs so far back she had her ankle chains caught in her earrings.

'I am truly sorry,' I said.

'It's okay. It's nothing,' she said.

She was plainly not going to say another word. I was loathe to leave. She was unlikely to visit me at lunch times, and I could hardly go and sit in her dental surgery and make small talk while she sat by a patient mixing up her filling materials, or whatever she does.

Together, Sue and I were the most talkative people I knew but now everything seemed either too trivial or too big.

I took an interest in the artwork on her walls.

'You can't beat landscapes,' I said.

Silence.

'These are very well done. See the spaces on the paper? Sometimes it's what you don't paint that counts. You've got to let the canvass shine out. It brings the picture to life.'

Surely she was too polite to let me talk without eventually joining in.

Silence.

'These are great,' I said sticking with the pictures.

Silence.

'And a good balance, the way you've put them in the room.'

'They're Ricky's. I hate them. You think they're good? I hate the bloody things.' She sighed. 'Oh, maybe they are good. I don't know.'

Rick wandered back in. He'd forgotten something.

I hadn't realised how irritable I was. The whole situation

came out of nowhere.

I looked at Rick and said, 'Look mate you've got to start treating Sue right, you know.'

'What do you mean?' he asked.

'You can't go hitting people. You can't just grind the poor woman into the ground. Sue's fantastic and you're just treating her like an arsehole.'

Sue was shouting at me. 'Get out of here David. Get out now. I am sorry Rick. He's completely out of order.'

'But he's an arsehole Sue, what do you think you're doing with him?'

Rick hit me very very hard in the face.

The last words I heard as I went down were Sue repeating, 'I'm so sorry Rick. Rick I'm so sorry. David get out of here. Get out of here.'

MIKE

There should have been lots of flashbacks; snippets, images I'd previously seen. We should all have slapped our brows and gone 'Of course! Bruce Willis was dead all along!' But there was nothing. Nothing tangible in the past to suggest that Chrissie had been married and I should have spotted it.

She was better dressed than perhaps I should have expected, but otherwise didn't have the trappings of someone married to a bit of money. Conversely there was the fact that she hung out with some pretty dire Fen folk; but then she was brought up there. It was one of those things that sort of made sense but nonetheless didn't feel right.

I paced around the kitchen trying her mobile number, reading it from a scrap of paper that said clearly, 'Chrissie's mobile' then the number.

I'd hear 'The mobile phone you are trying to reach may be turned off.'

I'd flick furiously through my address book muttering, 'Now I know why I haven't got a land line number for her.'

Chrissie arrived at my door. She'd been to the cheese shop in the centre of town and cycled back with fresh bread and olives and a preposterously obscure goats cheese. She explained this as she put it in my fridge. She didn't mention anything difficult. She looked energetic and innocent.

'Before we have lunch, come for a walk with me,' she said.

It would be a crucial conversation, dull even. Evidently this would be alleviated with clichéd Cambridge landmarks in the background.

'I never lied to you. Not once,' she said.

'That's not the point.'

'It's exactly the point.'

'I once asked why I shouldn't pick you up at your place and you said because it's a tip.'

'It is a tip.'

'But that's not why you didn't want me to see it.'

'How do you know?'

'How long have you been married?' As I asked this, King's College chapel loomed over my right shoulder.

'Four years,' she replied, the Catholic Church clearly visible behind her.

'Are you happily married?'

'Really that's my own affair.'

'Are you hoping to leave him?'

'What do you think?'

'I don't know,' I said.

We were suddenly in another street altogether. In the background, men stripped to the waist were punting down the Cam while women in flowing summer dresses lay back clasping Champagne. In one boat a Japanese tourist got his pole stuck in the river bed. He tugged at it, then the boat drifted out from under him, and he fell in.

'You have no right to expect me to answer these things,' said Chrissie.

'I have a right to safeguard my health.'

'A what?'

'I wouldn't want to catch anything.'

Chrissie's reaction showed she knew how bogus and insulting I was being. She hit me. She then kept talking in the same tone as before.

'It's called trust, Mike,' she said. 'How can I trust you, if I don't know you?'

Chrissie stopped dead. I had got to the crux of it.

'But Mike. You *do* know me. You know that I'm scornful, but kind, stylish but not trendy. I like films. I am reliable. You know that I'm straight, in both senses. I only laugh at your jokes when they're funny which isn't very often. You know that I'm cosmopolitan but proud of where I come from. You know that I like sex. You know amazing, lurid details about what I want sexually. Do you think for some magical reason it was easy for me to tell you those things? I let you penetrate my life in the most fundamental way possible and as far as you're concerned it counts for nothing.'

We walked on again.

'You know me, Mike.'

'But you're married,' I said.

'I thought you knew. Cambridge is so much like a village; I thought everyone knew everything.' She changed tone; more thoughtful now. 'I suppose he lives in London so much now, you might not have known.'

'I didn't know. Why does everyone keep telling me I should know things?'

'And it's my judgement call as to whether I'm available. I'll tell you something, Mike. I'm twenty-seven. I know a lot more about life than I did four years ago. You and I can have the perfect relationship. We're good for each other. We only do what we want to do; what we agree to do together. There is no downside. We have never let each other down; not once. How many couples can say that?'

'You're repeating your mantra too often Chrissie. You can't

use the same reasoning over and over.'

'Why not?'

'I don't know.' I laughed. 'It's some rule to being middle-class.'

I shrugged. Students in black gowns and mortarboards rushed past us hurrying to lectures.

I said, 'Look, you've heard of jealousy haven't you?'

'Look Mike, at this stage I'm looking for someone who doesn't open me out all the time. I'm looking for someone who loves me. Me.'

'You?'

'Yes, not Mrs Adam Hedges, wife of Mr Adam Hedges. Not Miss Christine Barrio daughter of a Fen big shot.'

'Why?' I asked, 'who is your father?'

'Every married person knows the difference between being known for who they are, or being known as part of a couple. You know me. Me. How can I put it? You know me.'

'Who is your father?' I asked again.

'Julio Barrio.'

We walked on.

'Oh surely you knew that at least?' she said. 'He owns half the town you work in.'

DAVID

We're now about ten days before Ray's death, and 35 before Chrissie's. My life was still hopelessly trivial.

I got to the office to discover that Julio had wanted me out at the bypass.

When I first joined the paper, we filled endless column inches campaigning to have a bypass for Reapham. We printed the press releases from the action group in favour and the various local councillors would wander into my office wanting to get their names in the paper, and be seen to support the cause.

But now it's all different. The construction company have started work on the road and we're all against it. There's too much disruption to local business. Farmers' land has been cut in two; it's difficult to get farm vehicles off to the mill, and the hidden cost to local business will be too great as cars no longer go through the High Street.

I still hadn't got my car sorted out so I cycled out to see the protesters.

I found them all easily enough. There were the hard-core half dozen who were against everything, including one or two who I was sure had campaigned to have it built in the first place. There was Julio looking very frenetic about something and, as if to make up the numbers, there were about forty Poles.

'Got your camera, David?' asked Julio.

I was wearing it round my neck so presumably it was rhetorical.

'What's the story Julio, and why are the Poles all here?'

'They are outraged citizens, David.'

'Why are they outraged?'

'Because they have to take their lives in their hands when they walk out to have a simple drink at the local pub. They work hard... are you getting this all down David?'

'I can remember it so far, Julio.'

'Make notes anyway. This is a legitimate story.'

'Your stories are always legitimate,' I said truthfully. Well, quite truthfully.

'The Poles are hundreds of miles from home and they work hard and they deserve to be able to drink in a good local English Pub,' continued the Italian.

'But you take them by coach to the pub.'

'I'm going to need to, now.'

I strode around taking photos. The road was half completed and we'd found a section not open to the traffic. We put lots of dejected looking Poles on one side of the road. Julio was trying to dragoon them into looking thirsty. I then went to take a picture of the pub they were trying to get to but Julio butted in.

'Not that one!'

'Why?' I asked. 'It's the nearest pub to their accommodation.'

'Yes. But it's not the one they'd aim for, because it's not the best.'

'You want me to take a picture of one of *your* pubs?'

'I run fine establishments and the Polish are a nation of people who understand good drink. Where do you think they would head for? Did I tell you that we now serve a beer made entirely from the barley grown in fields with crops circles?'

'I believe I'm running a story about it this week,' I replied.

Julio had two Poles standing with him: the three of them leaning against Julio's Ferrari. I had been told they were the two best English speakers but I had my doubts.

'While I'm here,' I asked, 'Do you know anything about the flying bits of car down at Reach Roots?'

The two Poles looked at each other and chatted a little in low voices. As if I would be able to understand them if they weren't whispering.

'It was a miracle,' said one at last.

'In what way?' I asked.

'They came from the clouds. There is no other explanation.'

I raised an eyebrow.

Julio spoke. 'I don't think that story got enough prominence,' he said.

'It was on page 5,' I said. Right hand pages get read more than left hand pages, so it was pretty prominent.

I'd done the best I could with the piece but I couldn't even write the 'police are baffled' because they hadn't even turned up. No crime had been committed. And the photo of an upturned seat piercing my windscreen somehow didn't work when we got it developed.

Julio's car started to move.

It's easy to understand the initial movement, if the handbrake had been left off and three grown men were leaning against it, it was likely to shift a bit, but once it had moved away from them it kept going. Uphill.

We watched. Idly at first, because we all assumed the car was going to stop. However, to my eye at least, it might even have been gathering momentum. Certainly it showed no sign of slowing. Okay, it was a Fen hill: we're not big on hills round here - stand on tiptoe and you get yourself a view - but nonetheless there was no getting away from the fact it was going uphill.

The other Poles fell silent and watched. The half dozen protesters looked nonchalant. They were determined to find nothing about this bypass surprising.

The Pole standing nearest me began to run after the car. The second one looked at me and Julio, then decided he was best off with his friend and ran after. I thought at first they were going to try and stop the car, but when they caught up with it they ran alongside cheering and waving it on.

The Ferrari kept going at a steady speed but was beginning to veer to the left. Another ten yards and it would be off the road. This motivated Julio to start running too.

'Stop it!' he was shouting.

I took a photo of his retreating body, his little legs ablur as he scurried after his car.

RAY

Some of the drivers are putting baby alarms in with their freight. So they can listen for immigrants in their trucks. Some of them are taking photos of their seals. I can't see how this works, but they love telling me about it.

There's a new regime where Immigration are putting probes into the freight to test for the levels of CO_2. If the CO_2 is high, then someone is breathing on board. But what about drugs? I know I will look sweaty and guilty at the port and I have done everything right. I have done everything I could.

They can smell guilt so they will pull me over. They may recognise me from previous trips. They liked me before and trust me. I'm one of them. They check the straps. They check where I'm going. They will seem happy. It was just something routine. I've had them climb all over the lorry. On the roof. Definitely customs men on the roof. I've seen trucks next to me have all their load removed. I've seen them take off the panelling. I run over this in my mind, over and over. I'm not even at the port yet but I'm in such a state.

I sit in the ferry and everything is fine but the hours last forever. I can't eat. I expect them to Tannoy me by name. They take a photo of me as I drive abroad. They take a photo of everyone. This is their evidence. Yes it was me, I'll say. I was driving the truck. I did everything.

I try to read the paper. But I have trouble reading. I can see the pictures, but I can't read the words. I can start a sentence but I can't concentrate enough to get to the end of it.

We are at Dover and this should be it. It isn't it. The bow doors are open and we should be moving, but we're not. Do we always take this long but I never notice it? When did I last drink? Drink tea, drink anything. I didn't eat, but I should have drunk.

The driver behind me is restless. He gets out of his cab and walks forward to me. He asks me what the hold up is. I shrug. I don't speak. He walks forward and soon returns.

'It's a protest.'

'What sort of protest?'

'The truckers aren't getting off until they've had their trucks checked for stowaways. But they're asking for trouble. This lot would fine you just for having a non-standard tank.'

I want to ask what a standard and non-standard tank would be, but stop myself. I used to try to talk to people like this. I used to go to truck stops. I would listen to other truckers, to learn their idiom, to learn to drop words like 'idiom.' But it never worked.

The trucker starts talking about O licences and tachographs.

'I've had a dreadful month. I was bloody locked up for six hours and had my tacho taken away. Then a month later I got done for not getting my tacho in by 21 days. Well I couldn't, could I? The bloody police had it.'

'Why what did you do?' I ask. He appears not to hear, so I say, 'Why what you done then?' then hate myself.

'I saw a lad hanging round my trailer at Maidstone and I chased him away and I rang the police. And I only said he might've come off my trailer. Might've.'

The trucker goes on and on but I can't hear the rest of what he says. I'm too nervous.

Scooby and Shaggy never learn they would be best off sticking with the others when walking round the disused fairground. Homer Simpson might realise he's stupid several times every episode, but he won't spend the next series attending night school.

This reflects a general truth: character progressions over a matter of weeks, a phenomenon so loved by novelists, are very rare indeed. If people do change, it tends to be slowly or not at all.

I say all this to console myself that I was unlikely to start cleaning my flat on a regular basis.

The carpets were beginning to squelch. Dark permanent drips were appearing halfway down the walls. I never flick fluids at walls. Which is what made it so scary.

I had been eating at work but had given myself a talking to, and as a result had developed a cunning two-pronged strategy to reinhabit my flat. So that I could eat breakfast, I went out and bought some bowls and kept cereal and milk in a corner of my bedroom. To keep the milk cold, I dangled it on a string out of my bedroom window. The downside of this innovation was that my bathroom sink was already full of cereal bowls with Cheerios spot welded to their rim.

The second prong of my strategy was more disastrous. I

acquired a toasted sandwich maker.

Now what I love about the toasted sandwich maker is its fundamental honesty. Take the humble cheese sandwich. Fresh soft bread smelling of yeast, slices of aromatic cheddar. Put those same ingredients in a sandwich maker and the true artery furring nature of the beast soon emerges. Fat the colour of bile and the willpower of lava begins to seep immutably from the edges and down on to the carpet. Or so I remembered too late.

Eating, washing and shaving at work had gone from being an option to being a necessity.

I was eating my breakfast: a cuppa soup at work when the news came through that a local TV news wanted to do a piece on our gravity defying hill. It was nearly a week after the original event because they'd spotted the story in our paper.

Julio commandeered me to show an interest. I was to get in on the act and try to raise the profile of the Reapham Gazette.

Before going out there I went across the road to see if I could talk to Sue.

Emma on reception looked doubtful.

'She doesn't want to talk to you,' she said.

'Where is she?'

'In the surgery with Mike. A patient has just thrown up. Mike hates vomit. Really really hates vomit.'

Mike is the archetypal dentist. Well-groomed, mild, probably plays golf; kind but dull and a little prissy. He tries to add a bit of self-conscious trendiness in to the mix but it strikes the wrong note. Wrong octave. Wrong everything.

If I were to nominate someone to draw him it would be Steve Appleby: a small well-meaning head, a nebulous body that has flowed down into his arse; his hands perpetually in his pockets to stop it seeping further down his legs. If this man relaxed any more he'd be comatosed.

The door to Mike's surgery opened. It was propped open by

a bucket. Sue was wielding a mop. The stench of vomit was almost visible in the air. I could see a harassed Mike in the background trying to clear up.

Sue picked up a couple of impression trays that had been dropped and threw them at Mike.

'No one talks to me like that,' screeched Sue. 'I know I'm not very good, but I'm not going to get any better if you keep shouting, I'm just going to get more nervous, and besides none of the other staff are prepared to work with you because it's so stressful, so you're stuck with me.'

Sue turned and saw me. She moved the bucket and shut the door.

I sat wondering what I could do next. If I sidled out, I'd look pathetic.

I sidled out.

Julio and Matt were in attendance at the bypass before the camera crews arrived. So were half the children of Reapham. They had got themselves a range of objects: supermarket trolleys, go-carts; even an old bowling ball. The kids were going up and down the hill, pushing each other, riding their bikes, whatever. It was very Giles.

Julio was dancing around with a spirit level that must have been about two metres long, biffing anyone who got in the way.

'I'm trying to find the true angle of the road,' he said. By which he meant he wanted to find the steepest part.

Matt was pushing the supermarket trolley up the hill; he had one arm in a sling from his ladder accident so he was doing well. The moment he let the trolley go, it ran back down the hill in a half hearted semi-circle. Julio was angry with him.

'Try the go-cart,' said Julio, 'and push it.'

Matt mumbled something under his breath. The TV crew was due any second. This was going to be embarrassing.

'I've got a five degree incline,' said Julio, 'but you have to make sure they measure it here.' He had marked out an area with chalk.

I was worried. 'Look,' I said, 'Is there any chance we were all mistaken. I mean the three of you were leaning on that car. Perhaps it was just a fluke.'

Matt went flying past, pushing a home made go-cart. He let go. It slowed up considerably then knocked over a small child.

There was a team talk. Justine was commandeered to drive the go-cart. She was the lightest there: the most likely to defy gravity. She lay flat on the boards with the string in her hands, her neck set at the same angle as the road. They had another trial run with Matt pushing hard, his stumpy little legs trundling up the hill. Justine's summer dress billowing up and her hand slapping it down for modesty's sake.

They crashed. Splintered board somersaulted. Wheels spun. Justine cartwheeled past us at shoulder height.

An argument broke out.

'I can't steer and hold on at the same time,' Justine was saying, apparently unscathed.

'Stick it in your teeth then,' replied Matt.

Another go-cart was found.

At that moment the TV crew arrived.

Julio's face turned to thunder. 'David, do something,' he hissed. 'We've got the idiot pushing that pram woman around. We're going to be a laughing stock. Have you any idea how hard it is to get even the local news interested in Reapham?'

A female TV reporter got out of the van. She looked far younger than me which was deeply irritating. There was a rancid seen-it-all sort behind her with some equipment; he must have been in his fifties but looked older.

I turned to Julio. 'Have you thought about using your car again?' I asked.

Julio got palsy.

'I don't think that's a good idea,' he said.

We looked at Matt pushing his girlfriend for a second time on the go-cart. Her hair got caught in the wheels. Her mouth twisted with terror. Her chin was still in her chest, but her head was cricked, shaking rhythmically, at a right angle. Matt leant forward to help but got his own hair caught in the wheel. It didn't occur to him to stop.

'We'll try my car,' said Julio.

We looked at his car. It had sustained a lot of damage on its passenger side. Painful gashes ran along the paintwork from the headlight all the way down to the rear indicator. There was a fold in the door by the handle where the metal buckled in and then protruded beyond the doorframe.

A slow tear emerged from the Italian's left eye.

I bowed my head in respect.

The reporter talked to me about what we'd seen previously. Julio was peculiarly quiet during the interview, nervous about his car, but he was given to dramatic exhalations when he felt I was selling the story short.

The day was going so badly that I steadily distanced myself from the story. I said, 'It could have been a fluke. After all, it was only one car.' When Julio heard this, he developed such an alarming range of breathing disorders that the reporter offered him some water.

The TV crew decided to take some establishing shots of the countryside, while the reporter went off to encourage the children to look busy. Julio was seething.

'Right,' he called, 'let's get this show on the road.'

'You might want to steer the car this time,' I said, 'to stop it crashing.'

'I can't steer it. It will look as though I'm driving it. That would make terrible TV.'

He was right of course.

'Well,' I said. 'Run along side and jump in and stop it if it goes towards the verge.'

The reporter had been listening. 'Sounds good to me,' she said.

They set up the cameras and Julio positioned his car.

'It was about here,' I offered.

Julio got testy with the TV crew. 'Don't film it from here,' he said. 'Film it from its good side.' His car had a good side.

They moved the cameras.

Julio took the handbrake off his Ferrari and we regrouped by the back of the car. The reporter insisted we were filmed answering one more question and then we were to lean as before on the car, and film it as it travelled up the hill.

The reporter's question was, 'This crop of recent phenomena at Reapham. Do you feel there's any chance they are being faked.'

I replied, 'Of course.'

Julio was so apoplectic his body bowed over. To steady himself he had both hands on the car. Churl that I am, I took this as my cue to push off.

The car moved away from us. Julio, who had done himself some sort of mischief, put both his hands on his knees to support himself while he got his breath back.

The car faltered about six feet from us. The reporter tilted her head with disappointment. I squinted. To my eye it hadn't quite stopped. Presumably it would in a second. I daren't hope that it would follow the same pattern to previously. But professional pride meant I wanted my fellow journalists to feel there had been some sort of story here. I willed that car to keep going.

It was still managing all of a centimetre a second, but undeniably it was moving. At that minuscule speed, however, it could stop instantly. It was now perhaps five yards from us.

There were some children ahead of it. I rushed off to clear them out of the way. One child was on a stationary go-cart, sitting talking to a friend. I pushed him forward, but he wasn't expecting it, so he fell backwards. My hand just caught the back of his head as it fell. His friend was standing gawping. He wasn't moving, but the car was getting close now, so I grabbed at him in passing. I was effectively steering the go-cart by pushing the lad's head while yanking, a touch too violently, on the other kid.

The car was now travelling at about a foot every two or three seconds.

The TV crew were alert to the fact that they might now have a story. The reporter stood erect. Her mouth open, her eyes narrowed.

Julio was the last to cotton on. His car was travelling quite centrally. But it was still too slow to tell if it would last the course without trouble.

Julio set off after it to make sure. As he ran, it gave a better sense of urgency to the scene, as if we really had something dangerous running away on us.The car was doing a good speed now. With a bit of editing we'd all escape with our pride intact.

Julio was worried about escaping with his car intact. It was heading for the edge of the road, where some heavy machinery had been left by the construction company building the road. If the Ferrari went that way then the other side of it would be dented.

Or the front.

Somehow the car had turned sufficiently to be heading for the shovel of a JCB.

Julio scurried. He got to the front of the car and turned to face it. He pushed with both hands on the bonnet, as if trying to push it back down the hill. Julio is not a large man, so his legs were pushed back at first. He was prepared to lose his life. Squashed between the car and the JCB rather than suffer another scratch on that car.

I looked at the cameraman. As far as I could tell, this little man in a cream suit and Eraserhead hair struggling backwards against his car had been captured perfectly on film.

I walk off the street and into the cinema. I pass a poster that says, 'Late Night Showing: Dead Romantic.'

I buy a tea in the foyer: it's in a large Styrofoam container with one of those tiny straws you use for stirring. I buy it with surprise in my voice that I would be able to buy it at all.

I sit on my own in the cinema. The first couple of scenes come and go. Extreme violence is served up with nonchalance. The people involved are miserably poor but have been filmed so beautifully it looks glamorous. Then the famous scene comes up where the actor Matthew Peck sits in a cinema on his own: he's watching True Romance.

I blow into my tiny straw so that tea lathers up in bubbles set against the brightness of the cinema screen.

Matthew Peck does the same on screen, but it's some other drink. His bubbles are bigger than mine.

On screen, the cinema exit opens and Julia Kilmer enters in a tight white dress holding a large box of pop corn. She has a four pack under her arm. Matthew Peck doesn't look round. She sits down three rows behind him.

In my cinema the exit opens but I don't look round. Matthew and I continue blowing bubbles.

The girl on the screen throws a piece of popcorn at Matt. A piece hits me on the ear. We blow bubbles again.

Another piece of popcorn hit me and Matt.'Oh I'm sorry,' says a voice three rows behind me, and up on the screen in front of me. 'Jesus I'm so clumsy,' say Chrissie and Julia in unison.

There's a silence on the screen and in the cinema.

Julia and Chrissie throw another piece of popcorn.

'What are you doing?' say Matt and I.

'What am I doing?' say the women.

'Yeah,' we say.

'What?' they say.

'This.'

'You know, it's always this and it's always that,' say Julia and Chrissie.

Chrissie throws a can of beer up through the air, cutting through the projection beam; at the same moment Julia does it. Matt and I catch the cans of beer cleanly.

'You're cute,' cry Matt and I.

'I'm beautiful,' return Julia and Chrissie.

'Yes,' we reply, 'isn't it lucky?'

On the screen a member of the audience tells Julia to be quiet. We wait. Silence from our own cinema. Chrissie and I cry from disappointment.

'Be quiet,' says someone at last.

'Yay!' I go.

Chrissie scampers down to my seat pulling her white dress into shape as she goes.

'Bravo,' I said. 'I didn't know you'd seen this before.'

'Mike, this is such an obscure film, I've had to see the bloody thing two nights in a row. The second night I had to bring a torch to make notes.'

Chrissie was very pleased with herself.

'I thought you'd like that,' she said.

We watched the film for a while, but Chrissie became restless. She stuck her hand forcibly down my trousers. My squeal matched a squeal from someone in the film.

Chrissie found my cock and squeezed it hard. She was eating my ear.

I brushed her away. 'I love this bit,' I said.

On the screen, the actress said, 'I'm standing before you as an ordinary person. Can you love a girl like me?'

RAY

There is a claim in the papers that some Chinese communities in Britain are seen as no-go areas by the police. The Chinese don't report their crimes such as theft or murder. They just sort it out themselves. If necessary people get killed. But none of them will talk to the police. The police deny this. Politicians deny this. Officially the Chinese communities have one of the lowest crime rates in the country. Go figure.

A famous American comedy actor is conned into buying a car 'that never runs out of fuel.' The actor, who earns a million dollars per episode for his New York based sitcom, sacks his publicist for 'failing to show his life in the proper light.'

There is a gangland shooting in a Manchester Nightclub. The police interview the 800 people present. 340 claimed not to have seen anything, while 460 people were in the toilets when the incident occurred. This last story is similar to the Chinese one so instead I opt for something more sordid.

This quite similar to the Chinese story, so I decide to do for a different article. An easy one.

The Harold Shipman case was splashed over several pages again. The biggest serial killer Britain has ever known. The number of women he murdered is in the hundreds. No one seems to know why he did it. People don't even seem to care. We don't seem to know about the victims. What were they like when they were young? Who were the grieving relatives and friends? Still, an easy one for me to remember today. Chinese, never ending fuel, mass murderer.

One of my daughters is turning sixteen. I buy her a watch; I take a trip to Cartier no less. I choose it and have it engraved on the back. 'To Louise with love Dad.' I arrange to see her through Jeanie's sister Claire.

I turn up at Claire's house at the appointed hour. I knock on the door but there's no answer. I wait and knock again. I walk a little back from the house and look up at the windows for some sign of life. There's no apparent life. I stand for a while. Perhaps she's held up somewhere. Perhaps she's struggling to get home. Waiting for a bus. Stuck in a traffic jam. I try to remember when I last saw Louise and how she seemed then. I knock again.

I stand waiting and my palms feel sweaty against the paper wrapping of her present. I go and sit in my car across the road. I'll wait. I can wait. They can't avoid coming home forever. Is this how my relationship with my daughter ends?

I wonder what Jeanie must have said to Louise over the years, what Claire must now be saying to her; whether her opinion of me is permanently coloured, whether she never got told of all the hard work, the day after day trying to keep food on their plates, the sixteen hour days, but instead she got told the half per cent where I shouted, or hit Jeanie, or told her she was fat?

An hour has passed sitting in my car, and still no one has arrived. I relive the conversation where we organised this date. Did I make it clear it was this Saturday? Was it misconstrued as a week later? No, we mentioned the date. I find an old biro on the floor of my car and I write on the present. I walk up to the front door and put the little box through Claire's door. I feel deep inside that this is the last time I will ever see this house.

MIKE

The phone rang and it was Chrissie.   She was very businesslike.

'You know your trouble?'

'No Chrissie. What's my trouble?'

'You don't engage.   You always look on from a distance. The rest of us don't have that luxury.'

'Okay. And this is?'

'A convoluted way of asking a favour.'   She started laughing.

'Convoluted and aggressive?'

'Yep. Sometimes I just need help, Mike.   Sometimes you should just give me that help without asking.'

'Okay.'

'Well today I need your help. Today I need to feel that you would do anything for me and that you would just support me even though you won't feel good about it.'

'Okay.'

'The thing is, we've broken down in a car.'

'That's it? You've broken down in your car?'

'It's not my car. We're at a service station in Norfolk.'   She gave the directions.

After I put the phone down, I checked on a map where I was supposed to be going and it turned out to not be in Norfolk at all, it was much closer, and in the opposite direction. I muttered to myself that we had a relationship where asking even mediocre favours seemed to be a big deal.

By the time I got there, it was dark and cold. It was one of those motorway service areas where there's a shop and a restaurant - brackets not twenty-four hours brackets - and a petrol station. There was no sign of Chrissie.

I queued up to buy something to drink in the indentikit shop. There was row upon row of the same chocolate bars and crisps that you see you in every petrol station in Britain. For all I know, they are even put out on the shelves in the same order.

There was a lad serving who must have been about twenty. He was pale and puffy with a bit of acne. There was one spot in particular that was bothering him low on his right cheek. It was weeping, and every so often he bent his head to the left to mop it on the shoulder of his T-shirt. Behind him, what looked like his manager was putting a plaque up on the wall. The plaque said 'Investor In People.' Heavy investment would indeed be necessary.

They had a second plaque already up. 'Motorway Service Station of the year award 1996.' Underneath it, in brackets, was written 'Harlow Area.'

'Given that this is probably the only motorway service station retailer in the Harlow area, its amazing you haven't won that award more often,' I said.

The youth looked at the plaque but there was no flicker in his torpor.

I wandered out and I could see Chrissie walking towards me in the gloom. She looked serious or nervous or distracted. She was wearing nondescript clothes; black trousers, a dark coloured top of some sort. She stopped short and just stood in front of me. The swoosh of intermittent traffic made our conversation staccato.

'Hi,' she said.

'Hi.'

She said, 'You know I've just spent ten minutes in the car doing my make-up. To see my own Dad.'

'I'm not your father.' I shrugged. 'You look great,' I said.

Then, of all people, the Monkey on a Stick appeared; he was in the car park some way away walking towards us.

'Shouldn't he be in prison or something?'

She shrugged.

He had a blue cast on his arm. All the hair on his head had been shaved of, but it still wasn't washed so there was scurf or lice eggs in the millimetre or so of greasy black stubble.

'What have you done?'

He looked blank.

'To your arm,' I said.

He stopped to consider the question. 'I was taking a picture up a ladder, and I fell off and my dad stood on me.'

'So what are you doing?' I asked.

Chrissie said a very Chrissie thing. 'We're smuggling drugs.'

And that made it all right.

'I owe,' she continued, 'these people a largish sum of money and they're going to wipe it clean if I do them a couple of jobs.'

I waited. There was evidently more.

'I have to go up to the coast and get a package and bring it back down. It's that easy.'

'You're drugs running?'

'Yeah. To feed my chronic drugs habit.'

'Really?'

'No, not really.'

I couldn't be bothered to answer that.

She said, 'I just figure it's the sort of thing you'd expect me to say, seeing as you think the worst of me. Look, if I'd known you were going to be like this...'

'Like what?' For some reason I looked to Matt for support.

Matt was pulling at nasal hairs and inspecting them. This was the one part of his anatomy he didn't object to grooming. He pulled at a particularly tough hair. It finally gave but when he inspected it, it had a bogey on it which he cleared from the hair by running it through his teeth.

'I'm not acting like anything,' I replied.

'The engine fell out the car,' said Matt.

'What?'

'The engine I put in. Well it didn't fall out, but it's not good.'

'Look,' said Chrissie, 'I wouldn't ask if I wasn't desperate. You know that.'

'I don't know anything,' I replied. 'What exactly are we doing here?'

'Matt can't drive because of his arm, so I'm driving but we've broken down.'

'Okay,' I replied. 'It's just it seems to have been made into a big deal somehow.'

'You're going to help us then?'

'Sure.'

Matt and Chrissie looked round for my car. I pointed it out.

'You'd better tell me where we need to go,' I said.

DAVID

'On your regional News at six thirty. Gridlock as animal protesters take to the streets of Cambridge. The report is published into the Pulham Hospital organs-for-cash scandal. Further disturbances at the Oakenheath Immigration Centre and (pause, changing to light hearted voice) the Reapham residents who defy gravity.'

We were crowded round the television in Julio's pub waiting for the news. To appear in the trailer thirty minutes before the main programme added to the general sense of festivity and lengthened the queue to the bar.

All the usual suspects were there: Julio, Justine, Matt and Matthew, the Poles. For all we knew there would only be a minute of us on the TV but we were going to base an evening's drinking round it.

During the wait, Julio asked me about Sue.

'Oh,' I said. 'I'm afraid I upset her. She's still not talking to me.'

'You should pursue her,' said Julio.

'She's only a friend. If she wants some space, I should respect that.'

'There's no such thing as only a friend,' said Julio.

I laughed. Sensing Julio was in a good mood I said, 'Tell me Julio...'

'Yes?'

'How can I put this?' I said. 'I live in a lovely little world which is almost cartoon like.'

'Okay,' said Julio. He found this amusing.

'In cartoons, you tend to know who the villains are, and the good guys, from the moment you see them. Cartoons are never whodunnits.'

'Okay,' he said.

'You see,' I continued, 'In a small community, you tend to know who does what, and what everyone is like.'

'Like in a cartoon!' said Julio to show he was following the gist.

'So, we've had crop circles with people dressed up like aliens, we've had bits of car flying off the top of a factory that you happen to own. I just can't help feeling you're involved.'

Julio chuckled away.

'David, let me tell you something. I love life. I really really love life. I love it that in England you can play huge practical jokes and no one minds. So I can see what you think. Dress the Poles up as aliens, perhaps. But I'd have a lot of trouble making cars run up hill. And why would I do these things?'

'I looked into the town of Devizes.'

'Okay.'

'And since they've had their rash of phenomena their tourism has gone up forty percent.'

'Oh we can do much better than that,' said Julio. 'We're starting from such a low base. People should come out from Cambridge and Newmarket, from Peterborough. A bit of lunch and drink...'

'So you are behind it all?'

'Oh questions, questions.'

'I'm a journalist Julio. I have a duty to educate and inform. I need to understand things.' This was a trifle pompous from a man who just that morning had penned a 'News in Brief' item that read, 'A rake was stolen from a garden shed in Swavesey. Police are said to be investigating.'

Julio waved me away. I was going to object then realised that he meant the local news came on. The pub hushed.

Evidently our paper had missed a story about some drunken local lads breaking into the back of the Immigration Centre and picking fights with the asylum seekers. It begged questions about the security down there. We'd have to look at that the following day.

Our news item about the bypass eventually featured. It had been given a jaunty air. Reapham residents (who obviously don't get out much) were shown enjoying the fuss of this phenomenon in a grass-chewing 'we eat raw onions' kind of way.

The footage, however, was undeniably dramatic. This white haired old man, impeccably dressed, was desperately trying to stop a car from running uphill. Such was its power.

Someone in the pub had taped it so we re-ran the footage. In the background you could see some idiot (me) cuffing a small child and pulling the hair of a second. While further in the background you could see Matt and Justine unleashing a flurry of slaps over each other's heads as they fell out about tactics for their go-cart.

At the office the following morning all hell broke out. Well, the phone rang a couple of times, which is our near equivalent. But it seemed to come on top of everything else. I had a splitting head where I'd had one drink too many at Julio's pub, and I appeared to have lost half my possessions.

There was a cartoon that I'd done a couple of weeks previously and which was now relevant enough to print, but I'd lost it. I was leafing half-heartedly through the ubiquitous piles of paper that form my office and became convinced that half my drawings had been nicked. But then it was all such a mess that I'd have said the same about bank statements or letters, or indeed the telephone.

The good news was that we were to be in the nationals. The red tops - the Sun, the Mirror etc. - were picking up on the story; even the broadsheets appeared to be keen. Even national television. The TV footage of Julio pushing his car had a certain jokey resonance. It was a hit.

Within a few days the scene out by the bypass had been transformed. A marquee had appeared from nowhere, presumably sanctioned by the farmer whose land it was on. There was field of about twenty tents, along with a pile of those eco-camper vans that new age travellers seem to favour: daubed in flowers and slogans about saving the planet while belching out possibly the foulest exhaust fumes of any vehicle this side of the Urals.

There were vans selling wholefood, crystals (lots of crystals) and healing tapes. There was a blackboard explaining where to go for various kinds of fortune telling and, most puzzling of all, there was a 'problem solving' labyrinth, made from wheat tied in bundles.

I wandered around getting a feel for the place. It was morning and a few travellers were sitting just outside their tents having an early morning fag. They wouldn't eat meat but they had no trouble with cigarettes, drugs, and as much real ale or Special Brew as it takes to shrink your liver to the size of a golf ball.

I'd agreed to meet some incoming journalists at eleven. They seemed to feel they could trust me, and to broaden their stories were looking at the crop circle photos and the articles I'd run on the flying car parts. I was their credible witness, God help them.

No doubt they would run articles featuring the travellers lying around their feet and fail to capture the flavour of local people all together. It made a pleasant change from the media showing Cambridgeshire countryside simply as Jeffrey Archer's place in Grantchester but there the good news ended.

Sue had agreed to see me. She hit the ground running. She was mid sentence as she walked through my door.

'Bloody Rick! Sold my bloody car.'

'What?' I asked.

'I passed my test, right? I never thought I'd pass. My instructor was always very positive that I'd do alright but I thought that he was just being kind. He was probably nice to everyone. Certainly he was very nice to me; he said that he hardly ever worked through his lunch hour but he did it for me because he liked me. He even asked me out once, but I said no. I really liked him and he was good looking and he must have had a bit of money, but he was sort of a wimp really. Perhaps if he'd asked me a bit more, but he only asked once and then looked a bit embarrassed.'

'But the point is I passed,' she continued, 'and I don't think I made a single mistake all the way round. I went straight home afterwards to tell Ricky. He was sitting watching the box and he'd had a drink at lunch time and I thought he'd be pleased, heaven knows why, but instead he just kept interrogating me about all the things that I "must have done behind his back." Arsehole. Then he started getting really stupid and even said that he reckoned that I might be having an affair with my instructor or that he fancied me or something. Well that was barely worth answering so I told him how stupid he was and then he started calling me names back.'

'Well these things have a certain pattern to them and sooner or later I start hitting Ricky or Ricky starts hitting me, and you find yourself saying really stupid things, but on this occasion it all fizzled out - I think there was something we both wanted to watch on the telly - because we both ended up sitting together on the settee and I was holding a bag of frozen peas to my cheek, well actually not a bag so much as the last handful of a bag of peas that I found in the bottom of the freezer, and Ricky was moaning that I'd kicked him in the groin. He was like kind of puzzled.'

'Two days after that I was at work as usual but Ricky was stuck at home. When I got home my car was missing. When I asked him where it was he answered, cool as you like, "Oh I sold it."'

'I just couldn't believe it. At first there was a chance he was joking. So I asked him what he meant and he explained - again as cool as you like - that he had met someone in the pub, and he had offered Ricky money for it. I asked how much, so he told me and it wasn't half what I paid for it, because I bought it from the girl at work and it's only fair to give the going rate because it's not like she's got lots of money and I asked Ricky where the money was and he said he was going to buy a motorbike with it. I was getting more stunned by the minute, I asked him how he managed to sell the car without my signature but that's a stupid question really; my signature is easy to forge.'

'I can't remember what I did, or rather what I did first; I was crying and shouting and I was hitting him on and off all evening. This time though, Ricky didn't fight back or argue, he just sat there trying to ignore me and watch the telly. Eventually he said he was fed up with all this and he was going down the pub. I said fine and don't come back. When he'd gone I bolted the door so he couldn't get in again, and I bolted it properly because I'd always insisted that we have really good locks and stuff because you never know who's trying to do you some harm in this world.'

'So,' I said, 'You've chucked him out?'
Sue sat down next to me.
'Yeah. How old are those chips?' she asked.
'Two days or so,' I said.
They weren't that old, but I was hungry.
Sue said, 'That's disgusting,' and didn't eat any.

I parked my car with Chrissie and the Monkey on a Stick, in some lane in the middle of nowhere. I opened the car door to see if the car was on decent ground.

'No, stay in the car,' said the Monkey on a Stick.

'I had no intention of getting out.'

'Give me the keys.'

'No.'

'Give me the keys.'

'You little fuck arse. It's bad enough I gave you a lift. You're not having the car keys.'

The idiot greasy boy then came flying over the seats at me and pulled the keys out of the ignition. I grappled with him and pulled at his face. I had a look on my face that said I didn't mind fighting him but did I have to touch him?

I was furious. 'I've lost the keys now!'

We stopped fighting and both started looking on the floor of the car.

'I think they went outside,' he said.

Matt got out the car and disappeared into the gloom and I continued looking under the seats. Chrissie was wandering towards me through the darkness.

'I give the little tosser a lift and that's what he does. Where's he gone now?'

Chrissie shrugged.

'Well, help me look for the keys.'

'What do they look like?'

'You stoned or something? It's my keys. They look like keys. If we haven't got any keys then we're stuck here.'

Chrissie stood tall with her legs together. She lit another cigarette. I wandered off to look in the boot of the car for a torch which I thought I kept for map reading, but I couldn't find one.

'Where shall I look?' asked Chrissie.

'On the grass. I think they're on the grass.'

Matt wandered back. 'I've got a problem. Chrissie, you're going to need to come.'

'I'm looking for the keys Matt,' she replied.

'Yeah well, I've got a bigger problem than that.'

RAY

The man on the phone had told me where to park and it was well chosen, it is easy to get to from the motorway; down a little-used lane where there is a lot of woodland to hide in. I leave my rig and walk off to the pub that I'd been told was further down the road.

The barman doesn't spot me waiting. I appear to be invisible. Other people are served before me.

Eventually I order a meal and pay for a pint.

I sit and eat my meal and get out my paper. This is what I do, this is my habit. There is nothing in it I want to read. It must be the silly season.

A Hollywood actress won't let her boyfriend drive her new car.

A famous journalist turned cook has bleached her hair.

This is on the same page in a quality newspaper as a piece about our troops preparing to invade Afghanistan.

I just stare at it and stare at it. It makes no sense that I care about this so much. But I don't care about this. I feel calm. I feel calm because I know what I want to do.

I realise I have been playing with the newspaper. I have rolled it up and am tearing at it. No one in the bar cares that I do this.

I have pulled the paper to shreds and now I telescope it. I

last did this as a child. Or for my children. It looks like a tree or a firework.

I take an individual strand of the paper and tear squares of it away. I have now got paper everywhere. On the floor. I have torn most of the paper now. I don't remember doing it.

I stand up and take the knife from my plate. I don't want to have to wonder when what pitiful amount that is left of my life will be fucked up further. I will walk out of the pub.

The knife is one of those second rate pieces of stainless steel cutlery that has a couple of half hearted serrations pressed into the edge instead of a proper blade. It will do. Maybe I'll just drive my rig off somewhere and leave it at that.

I assume that someone had been in the woods and had watched me arrive, so they have probably got their freight out already. It will probably make no difference if I take the truck early. This will avoid bloodshed. I'm over aware of the sound my feet make on the road. It is so dark that I have little alternative but to keep along it. There is a street light far in the distance well beyond the truck. I try to walk towards it. I figure that I can't see the road, but if I can see the light ahead there must be nothing between me and the light; nothing to bump into. This isn't going to help me if there are any potholes in the road. I keep going though, my hands by my sides.

I can see the truck, or rather, a light flickering around. I'm a lot closer than I thought. There's a little straggly man and a taller skinny woman. They seem to be able to open my cab with no effort. Perhaps this is the modification that has been made to my truck; an easy way of entering. They both climb up into the cab. The woman has the skinniest arse I have ever seen in my life.

Evidently they aren't happy. They're pulling at one of the compartments in the cab. I am right by the cab door now. I can't think of something appropriate to say, so I cough.

The girl turns her head round and glares me.

'What do you want?'

'What do you mean what do I want? You're in my truck.'

'Oh.'

The woman climbs out and stands by me on the grass. We look toward the cab together, as if we know each other. We both wait for the little one to come out, but he doesn't. He keeps bobbing around in the cab looking for something.

I climb up into the cab to haul him out by the neck. I shout at him to get out and I drag him out sideways across the seats. I slip on the edge of the door and drop like a stone. Initially I still have his neck in my hand and I feel something give in his neck as I fall and I feel the back of my head crack against the sill. I climb back up and realise for the first time that he's got some sort of cast on one arm. I drag him out of the cab and he's moaning about the pain or something and how I've got to be careful with him. Why? Why do I have to be careful with the little piece of shit? He's on the ground now and I put a foot on his neck. I must be about three times heavier than him. I push harder with my foot. I haven't thought of what I want to say yet. I move my foot to the arm strapped across his chest. I realise this isn't a plaster cast but merely strapped, there'll be more pain there when I push and the bonus of him being able to speak if I ask him any questions.

The straggly girl meanwhile just stands and watches so I don't know what planet she's on. She appears to be waiting for us to finish so we can all go home.

The scruffy one on the ground speaks first. 'What is it you want?' he says.

'I want to know what makes you think you have the right to fuck up my life.'

'What are you on about?'

'What do you think? You can't just fuck up my life. What

gives you the right to fuck up my life?'

The little ape man on the bottom of my foot doesn't seem to understand.

The girl speaks. 'He's just supposed to pick up the package and get it down to London. It's no big deal. He's just doing his job, like you're doing your job.'

'I'm not doing any fucking job freaky girl, I just want all you people to leave me in peace.'

'That's nothing to do with him is it?'

'Why not?' I ask.

'Look at him. Why does everyone think it's okay to hurt him?'

All the while I've forgotten that I had a knife on me. Now I've remembered it I still don't use it. It's alright to punch or kick someone or strangle people like this with your hands, but using a knife seems wrong, just like gouging out their eyes would be wrong.

Someone else has turned up. It's so bloody dark, and the torch they had seems to have fallen somewhere and gone off. Judging by what I can see and by his voice he's late twenties and quite well built.

'I know you can't see me clearly, but take me seriously. I have a shotgun.'

I keep my foot on the little one's arm.

'You. Matt. Have you got what you came for?'

Matt doesn't answer. The straggly girl decides that now would be a great time to light up a fag. This woman must have a serious problem with nicotine.

The man I can't see shoots his gun. He shoots it to his right, away from us and into the woodland. The flame from the end of the gun etches my vision. There's the cry from unseen birds.

'Matt, I'm serious. Talk to me. Have you got what you came for?'

Matt isn't answering.

'You. The trucker. Is there a torch in the truck somewhere?'

The skinny girl speaks. 'So you've been watching us in the dark?'

'Trucker,' persists the man with the gun. 'Have you got a torch?'

I've grown attached to the idea of having my foot on the ape man's broken arm and somehow I'd felt this gave me a bargaining position.

Don't shoot or I'll hurt the little scruffy one.

'I'll get a torch,' I offer.

I think I can hear the gun being opened for another cartridge. I get up into the cab and sit in it. If I run the engine I probably wouldn't be able to make a dash for it in time. He could shoot through the open door, or shoot at the tyres. He has such a good view. I'm the only thing he can see in relief against the dark. He can't miss.

I get the torch and climb down. I can see less than ever after the light in the cab. I turn on the torch. It is strong. I find I have no fear. Is it because I have not seen whoever has the gun? Has something died in me so that I no longer have fear. I conjure with it. I no longer fear death. I shine the torch on the imp. Everything seems to be far away. The imp isn't moving. Surely I haven't killed him. Whoever has the gun has gone quiet. He's wondering about the imp as well.

'Matt!' cries the man with the gun. He turns to me, 'What have you done to him?'

'I haven't done anything to him,' I reply.

I should be afraid. Afraid that in some way I have killed him, but I'm not. I pass the beam over him.

'Give me the torch.' He's trying to sound fierce but he's afraid.

I offer the torch into the darkness. He shines the torch at

Matt. Matt's eyes are shut. He is still. Now they are open. He still doesn't move. His eyes open wide, then they blink. The man with the gun is happy. He is shining his torch elsewhere.

'You! Chrissie. Where's the package?'

The straggly one is called Chrissie.

'Christine to you, Richard.'

The one with the gun is Richard.

'I want someone to tell me where the package is or I will start shooting.'

'Look. Can we just calm down a little?' I say at last.

Matt speaks, 'I couldn't find it.'

'Why were you so late getting here?' asks Richard.

'My car broke down,' replies Matt.

Richard turns the torch on me and walks closer to me.

'See this gun?' he says.

I am not going to answer him.

'I am going to use it. Because I have had enough. One of you must know where the package is.'

'Look, whatever it is you're looking for, if I'd removed it,' I say, 'I'd hardly turn up here, would I? I'd do a runner.'

Chrissie speaks. 'Look, if you've been watching all along you must have seen that we couldn't find it.'

There's still silence from Richard or Rick.

'Okay,' he says at last. 'I want your keys.'

I don't realise at first he meant me. He is getting increasingly uncertain and nervous so my silence makes him angry.

'Give me the keys. You! Trucker! Give me the keys.'

'Why?' I ask. I'm not going to give him the truck. What I actually say is, 'I can't give you all of my keys. There's my door key for a start. I'll need that, won't I?'

'Show me your keys,' he says.

I get them out and he shines the torch on them. Again he pauses.

138

'Okay, get your house keys off, then.'

He then takes the torch away, so I'm expected to do it all by Braille.

'Now Matt, Chrissie,' he calls.

'Christine, you arsehole,' says Chrissie. 'How did you two get here?'

'What's it to you?'

'I don't want you fucking following me,' he replies.

'Why would we want to follow you?' asks Chrissie. 'Are we gonna get paid by the way?'

'For doing what?'

'For doing our end of the bargain. It's not my fault there was nothing to pick up.'

'Just give me your car keys.'

'No.'

'Fine. I'll just shoot up your car. Where is it?'

MIKE

I was still on my hands and knees. A little light spilled out from the open door of the car, but not enough.

The shot went off, but it seemed some way off. I kept combing the undergrowth, moving backwards methodically.

A light was slowly appearing in the distance. A torch. Then three people were close to the end of the car. I was hidden behind the car.

A voice I didn't recognise said, 'Right now, the choice is I get the keys or I disable the vehicle.'

'Look,' said Chrissie. 'If we've lost the keys, we can't go anywhere can we? You can't just go around shooting people's tyres up and stuff, Rick, it's pathetic.'

I skulked in the darkness

Chrissie was reasoning again. 'I still don't see why you need to stop us getting home tonight.'

'I've got to have time to search that truck,' replied Rick.

'You're going to drive the truck away?' she asked.

'I can't search it and stop you lot from moving at the same time,' he reasoned.

'Can't you just trust us?' she asked.

'I don't trust anyone. If you lot have taken the package then I don't want you to be in a position to run off with it.'

The torch beam moved again. There was a crunch of twigs

and I stiffened. Someone was coming round the car towards me. I was still on my hands and knees so Rick must have had the sight of my arse in his torch beam. An arse shuffling off round the car in fright.

'Oi! Stop!'

I stopped. I still had my arse to him.

'Turn round.'

The arse turned round.

'What's happened to you?' asked the voice behind the torch.

I was aware of the cut along my jaw line. I was covered in mud and grass from fighting Matt.

We didn't get much further because the person I now know as Ray had come up behind Rick. He must have belted him round the head because the torch went flying and there was a gunshot that was aimed nowhere in particular. A ringing sound hung in the night, followed by the noise of birds woken in the woodland, and then the sound of a donkey braying. It was ridiculously close and, well, just not apt. A light went on in a house that seemed remarkably close.

Ray was a fat man but surprisingly strong. Ricky was quick and naturally vicious, but it was Ray who was the psychopath by nature. Ricky had the air of someone who did what he had to do, while Ray had the twitch and manner of someone with a psychological disorder.

Rick thrashed about and was all elbows and kneecaps. Ray was just solid; there was no wrestling him to the floor and he was too soft to dent.

Ricky then stopped moving; he was suddenly a lot more frightened.

'What are you doing?' he breathed.

'Move again and I'll take your neck off.'

Ray must have had a knife.

Ricky asked, 'What do you want?'

141

'I want to be left alone. I want to just do my job. I want to just have my life. I don't want any of this.'

'Er, should I stand up now?' I asked. I sounded very pathetic and middle class.

'Who exactly are you?' asked Ray.

I found this a difficult question to answer. I stammered a bit.

'I just drove us all here,' I said.

'What this one? You drove this one?' He meant Rick.

'No the other two. And now I've lost my keys.'

As if there was some kind of duty roster for who gets the power, or to keep some sort of unspoken rhythm going, the Monkey on a Stick ran forward and picked up the gun. Such was his excitement that he didn't say anything for a while. He kind of hopped up and down.

Rick said. 'Okay mate. Take that thing away from my throat, or Matt shoots you.'

But Ray was psychotic and not open to reason. Ray didn't give ground, and Matt didn't give ground, so there was a long wait where no one knew what to do.

Eventually I said, 'Do you mind if I crouch?'

'No,' replied both Matt and Ray.

There were lights in the distance as a car started its way down the road. Matt became agitated by this. He started hopping and twitching with extra frenzy.

'Look, you two move apart,' he said. He kept looking over his shoulder where the car was getting closer. He was going into spasms of worry.

'Put the gun carefully down,' said Ray who seemed to be relaxing into his role.

But the Monkey was getting more agitated looking at the car and looking back at Ray and Rick.

Then the Monkey started counting, 'Five!'

'What?' asked Ray.

'Four!'

'Oh come off it, you little turd, you'll just shoot your friend here.'

'Three!'

'Oh shit,' said Chrissie. 'Oh shit, oh shit, oh shit.'

Chrissie dived to the ground.

Rick started struggling left and right, trying to get himself out of the line of fire. The car was getting closer. The Monkey on a Stick was still counting.

'Two!'

Everyone froze momentarily. The fact that the Monkey stopped gyrating was too unnerving to bear. His hand was steady and he raised the gun up to the level of the two men's heads. Ray and Rick both dived to their right and the gun went off. The car passed sweeping its lights over us at the same moment.

Rick was shouting and went running over to Matt and was kicking him and punching him.

'Jesus Christ, Matt. What the hell do you think you're doing? Guns are bloody dangerous.'

Matt was on the ground and Rick was beating the crap out of him.

Ray, meanwhile, had picked up the gun. He stood there, assuming that by holding the gun he had power, but when Rick saw what Ray was doing he stormed up to him.

Ray pulled the trigger with a click and nothing happened, both cartridges were spent. He let Rick pull the gun out of his hands, and then simply watched as he took cartridges out of his pocket and reloaded.

'Right. Take your clothes off.'

'What?' asked Ray.

'Take your clothes off. Now.'

'Why?'

Rick explained himself. Evidently we couldn't conceal car keys if we were naked. This spurred Chrissie into life. She stood up and was dusting herself off.

'Rick, look, I understand what you're at here,' she said, 'but for one thing it's cold. And also, if you're worried we're going to come after you then believe me, we just all want to get home.'

'I don't want you lot to go anywhere. I've got to search that truck, but if I don't find what I want... look just take your clothes off.'

'Can't we at least keep our shoes on?' asked Matt.

'Oh fuck, keep your sodding shoes if it makes you all happy.'

Chrissie started lighting up her umpteenth fag. The group had become quite calm. Rick went up to Matt who made no attempt to keep his distance which was a mistake because Rick then put his arm around his neck and held his shotgun against the side of his stomach. We started pulling our clothes off.

Chrissie said, 'Mike hates being naked in front of strangers. I'm not sure why, Mike, it's not as though someone is going to point and giggle when they see your cock.'

Rick looked over and giggled. 'I don't think much of the size of yours,' he said.

Chrissie found this amusing.

Ray took his clothes off and I did the thing men do, where I appear not to look but check him out anyway by flicking my head past him to apparently glare at Chrissie.

Matt was looking bewildered. 'How am I going to take off my clothes with this cast on?' he asked.

'Take off your trousers then your pants,' said Rick.

The Monkey on a Stick tried to take his trousers of with one hand but failed.

'You, Chrissie, take his bloody clothes off would you?'

Chrissie, who has a fine body, wandered over. She's not self conscious. She was already shivering though. She got down on her knees and undid Matt's trousers. It was same pose as if she was going to give him a blow job. He had hairy, skinny legs and an above average cock sitting in a sea of black pubes. It was fair game for us all to look at Matt but not each other.

'Well hello,' went Chrissie. She pouted her lips at him before standing and moving away. Matt started scratching his leg and then he started playing with his cock. Chrissie started laughing.

Rick asked us to put all the clothes in one big pile. As I moved my clothes my keys got turned and made a chinking noise. They had been tucked in the grass not far from us. Everyone was too absorbed by Matt rubbing himself to hear them.

Matt was detailed to put the clothes in the truck. Matt needed a couple of trips to do this and when he'd finished Rick, who suddenly seemed anxious, disappeared off to the truck.

Rick drove the truck past us and I waited until it was out of sight before telling everyone that I had the car keys. I was watching the light of the truck deep in the dark. It was largely obscured by the woods now and there was a far off blue light by it, that was obvious but ill-defined.

Ray was cross. 'What? I've got to stand here stark bollock naked because you couldn't bring yourself to hand over the keys of your precious car.'

'I'd rather be naked but have a way of getting home,' I replied.

'We're going to have to go,' said Chrissie. 'I think that's the police.'

We looked into the gloom again and sure enough there was a blue flashing light. We scrabbled to get into the car. Chrissie hopped in beside me, and Matt and Ray had to sit in the back.

We had a quick discussion as to whether it made more sense

to drive towards the police and pass them so that they would have to turn in order to follow us. It seemed to me that if we went the opposite way then they wouldn't even have seen us, which given that we were all naked, was a bonus. I announced I'd drive us away.

This involved a tricky three point turn in the narrow road, with a ditch on one side and trees on the other. Four point turn. Five point turn. The police car was making steady progress towards us. I turned off our headlights. My companions started moaning that this had made the eight point, nine point turn all the harder. We could now see both beams of the police car clearly. It was about a hundred yards away but it was so impenetrably dark, they would have to get very close to identify us.

'They haven't stopped the truck then,' noted Chrissie.

My last couple of manoeuvres hadn't helped much. I revved up and just took my chances on the ditch and undergrowth on the far side and in a sweep that took in a couple of nasty bumps, a lurch down and a lurch back up again, where it sounded as though something in the car gave, we were away. I then tried to get it away a little faster with my nose pressed against the screen peering into the gloom.

The rearview mirror was shaky. The police didn't seem too close. The Monkey on a Stick started a animated commentary about the police behind us.

'They're not stopping, you know,' he said.

'Now the truck's gone and we're gone, there's nothing to see,' said Chrissie talking over Matt, 'and they won't be quite sure where they were supposed to be looking, so it's my guess they'll keep at a steady speed peering into the gloom for where the action is.'

'If it was reported as a shooting, shouldn't there be more than one car?' asked Ray.

'Perhaps it wasn't reported as a shooting. Anyway, this is the countryside. They can't mobilise the county's marksmen every time a farmer takes a pot shot at a rabbit.'

'Of course, they might stop,' I said, 'and talk to whoever reported the incident. A lot of police work is about making people feel good when they're worried about crime; when they report a crime, making them feel something is being done.'

Somehow the more I rationalised, the more stupid I looked, stark bollock naked with my nose spread against the screen, peering with big eyes into the night.

RAY

Not only do we have to put up with the fact that this idiot, Mike, has managed to get us all naked, but he is so noncy about his car that instead of fleeing as fast as he could, he's peering into the darkness looking for little potholes and stuff and piddles along like a granny learning to drive, right in the middle of the road. His car is built like a tank but has probably never negotiated anything more difficult than a school run. He probably gets in a panic if the mud flaps get brown.

We're well clear of the police car and Skinny Girl starts moaning that she's hungry and cold. The car's heater has us at about four hundred degrees, but in that fugged up kind of way you get in minicabs at night.

'Have we got any money between us?' asks Skinny Girl.

Unless someone is in the habit of sticking a few coins up their arse for just such emergencies, I'm thinking not.

'How far are we from home?' she asks.

Granny Driver reckons about half an hour. We drive along in silence but Skinny Girl is getting restless.

'Doesn't anyone care that I'm hungry and cold?' she says.

'How can you be cold?' I ask.

'I'm naked, you idiot. I haven't got the fifteen extra stone of spare flesh to keep me warm that you seem to have. Mike, look there's a supermarket, let's go down there.'

Granny Driver slows a little.

'What?' he says.

'Before we hit the A road,' she says. 'It'll be open. It's probably 24 hours. Let's have a look.'

'We haven't got any money.'

'Look just take us down there would you?'

We park by the windows of the store, because Chrissie wants to get away quickly if there's a problem. She sits for a while and thinks. The shop looks mostly empty. Very occasionally a car will draw up or a shopper will leave the store. We can see one cashier from where we are and she is not working. It's so quiet there's a cat wandering along.

'Okay, which of you is coming in with me?'

There's silence. Mike looks too sensible, and the greasy one is, well, who knows what's going on there but it doesn't involve anything rational.

'Mike?' she asks.

Mike is obviously absolutely besotted with this woman. He keeps his eyes trained on her every second he can. Despite this, he's still not keen.

'I'm not coming in there naked. I'm a dentist. Dentists don't do that sort of thing.'

Chrissie looks at Matt, then me.

'Come on Mike,' she says.

MIKE

'Why do you need anyone at all?' I asked weakly.

'To carry stuff.'

All I had were the rubber car mats that are on the floor. I held one car mat to my crotch and one over my arse, and got out of the car. Then panicked and got back in again.

I sat tight and grimaced at Chrissie.

Chrissie got out of the car. She was stark naked and walked tall. She didn't go in the store straight away, she went up to the cat that was hanging around and gave it a stroke. I sat there looking at her through the window of the car.

Chrissie picked up the cat and walked into the shop with it. I could see a few shoppers look in her direction; they were very matter-of-fact. The three of us shrinking naked in the car suddenly looked the stupid ones.

Chrissie reports that she first went off to look for the section that sold kitchen utensils to see if she could get a kitchen knife. She had to ask a member of staff the way. She couldn't find a knife so had to settle for a can opener. The kind with two handles and a butterfly shape you have to turn at the end.

She took the can opener and the cat to the nearest till. Chrissie was holding the cat away from her body in case it scratched her but it seemed quite happy. She held the can opener against the cat in the most menacing manner she could and started talking to the assistant.

'Hello, I want you to listen carefully to what I want. We need some clothing and we need some food. I am prepared to hurt this cat. But if I get what I need, I will not hurt this cat.'

Chrissie squeezed the two handles of the can opener together a few times to emphasise how serious she was. The cat looked content. The cashier looked blank.

'I can't leave the till,' she said at last.

A supervisor came over. He kept to the far side of the cashier so as to be only half involved.

He asked Chrissie what she wanted and Chrissie explained again. He had a cheap suit and a tie pulled over his paunch and tucked into his waistband. He was going to have to make a decision that was beyond the supermarket's very clear guidelines.

He went for honesty.

'You see, here's the problem,' he was trying to avoid eyeing up the naked Chrissie, so had his head half turned away, 'if you threaten a member of staff, we have clear guidelines not to put her in a dangerous position. If you shoplift, we have clear guidelines to chase and apprehend. But a cat? There's no rules for threatening a cat.'

They all looked at the cat. It was now purring.

'Yeah, but if I threaten the staff,' Chrissie pointed out, 'I'm guilty of a bigger offence.'

The three of them felt this was an impasse.

'What about,' said Chrissie, 'if I say, look if I'm prepared to do this to a cat, then just imagine what else I could do.'

The supervisor didn't look too imaginative.

'What about,' said the assistant, 'if what she says itself isn't too threatening but what with the cat having a whatever to its throat, it just tips the balance for you to believe you shouldn't take the *chance* of putting me in danger.'

'Well it hinges on whether you feel threatened,' said Chrissie. She leered at the assistant. 'Do you *feel* threatened?'

The assistant looked to her supervisor for the answer. The supervisor had sweat on his cheeks. He nodded. He turned to Chrissie.

'What do you want then?'

'Clothes.'

'Clothes?'

'Yeah, I'm frozen. I don't usually go round naked you know.'

'What sort of clothes?'

'Anything. Staff uniforms. Medium. No three medium and one large.'

Chrissie then itemised an assortment of snacks and drinks over and above her clothing request and the manager shuffled off.

'Oh and some food for the cat,' added Chrissie, 'in those foil packs so I can open it easily.'

A customer came up behind Chrissie with a basket of goods. He stood quite close for a while and dithered about putting his stuff on the conveyor belt. He put a bar across the belt indicating that he was the next customer, and then put down a carton of milk, but not the other items from the basket. There was no other cashier on duty, so he had few options, but after a while he took the carton back and put it into his basket and moved back a few feet and waited.

In the car, Ray was beginning to moan.

'She's fucking deranged. You know that don't you?'

'Yeah,' I replied, 'and so gorgeous.'

I looked at Ray in the rear-view mirror. I had a worried look. Eyes open, mouth inadvertently wide. Ray looked sweaty.

'She's taking far too long,' he said. He was chewing something imaginary. 'They'll be stalling her and calling the police. This is total lunacy. You're idiots, you know that don't you? Who is she anyway? Is she your girlfriend?'

I let him go on. He was right that there was an interminable wait, but eventually the supervisor returned with three bags. From her body language you could tell Chrissie had a dilemma. She was going to have trouble carrying the bags and the cat and the 'weapon'. She dropped the cat and ran with the bags. The moment she was away from the till there was an announcement over the intercom.

'Code Nine.'

Every able-bodied male member of staff came hurtling through the shop; three including the supervisor. Chrissie pelted for the way out which was one of those large revolving doors that stop dead if you push them. Chrissie pushed them. The chase was temporarily in slow motion. In one section of the rotating door was Chrissie, naked with her bags, marking time. In the section behind were two teenage shelf stackers, one out of breath from the five yard run and the other with a smile on his lips and a salacious look in his eye as he studied Chrissie's departing arse.

I revved up the car and leant over to push the passenger door open. One of the shopping bags hit me on the shoulder as Chrissie hurtled in. I tried to reverse but the gear stick got caught on something. There was a lot of pushing and shoving and we were going backwards as the two shop workers were running up to the car. One of them slapped their hand on the bonnet; bravado to show they'd got to the car on time. He then laughed.

They got out of the way as I moved forward and turned the car in a circle to get out of the car park.

We shot along, and needless to say made a bad decision on how to get out of the place. We looped round the car park looking for the wretched exit but kept taking the wrong turn. At one stage I even found myself caring that I'd gone the wrong way on a route marked 'Exit Only' with white paint on the ground. I could see the blue lights of a police car coming down a slip road. We drove up and out, straight past them, sinking ever deeper into our seats. The police seemed to be continuing down to the store.

Chrissie shared out her spoils, which included a bottle of tequila. She moaned that it was white tequila: the shop staff had skimped. Fat Ray was happy to struggle into his uniform as fast as he could, Matt just lay the clothes over him to keep warm. Chrissie played with hers. The store had put white hats in the bags: the sort butchers wear. Chrissie pulled down the mirror to check how she looked in one. She hadn't got round to putting on the other clothes yet, but was wasting no time getting down to some drinking and unwrapping a chocolate bar.

'They've even included different sizes,' she said. She tried on another.

'Do you think they got my registration number?' I asked.

No one answered. Chrissie started dispensing Snickers bars and offering up her bottle of drink.

I drove us onto progressively smaller roads and when we were in clear countryside I pulled the car over so that I could change into some clothes. Three of us were now sitting grimly in our butcher's uniforms.

'I suppose that's the end of it,' I said. 'Am I dropping people off home? Who lives closest?'

I took the car around and headed off for the A road.

'I've got to report my truck missing for a start. Perhaps I ought to go to a police station.'

'Dressed like that?' said Chrissie. 'When they're also looking for some people who held up that place?' Chrissie gave me a look on the subject of Ray's sanity.

'How about if I take you home?' I suggested.

It wasn't long before we discovered that Ray, Matt and Chrissie hailed from the same part of the Fen.

'So let's get this straight,' I said, 'For my benefit at least. You were carrying something in your lorry, but you don't seem very happy about it, and these two who are also from the same part of town as you, were detailed to take it on to the next stage of the journey. And you're all...' I was getting stuck already. 'So basically, the people who organise everything do it at arms length, but keep an eye on you lot who do the dirty work.'

Silence from the rest of the car.

'Ray, what were you carrying?'

'I have no idea. Rocks?'

'And what about Rick? He also lives out in the Fens near you lot?' I asked.

Silence again.

'Chrissie, do you know him?'

'No.'

'You're lying.'

'And?' she replied, she already sounded drunk.

'Matt, you know him. Where does Rick come from?'

'Sanity Row.'

'So, Ray here, Rick, and your mother are all near neighbours.'

'You're a bit over qualified to chauffeur us, aren't you Einstein?' replied Chrissie.

We drove for a while. No one was going to fill me in.

'Well it makes dropping everyone off easy enough,' I said at last.

'Look,' said Chrissie. 'This is what life is like. It's not some heist movie, with Freddie 'The Fingers' the safe cracker, and Mickey 'The Brains' McMobster. People just muddle through. They find little people who are desperate enough or stupid enough to do the little jobs, so the people who make the real money keep their hands clean. The people they use are bound to live close to each other - or likely to - because you can only choose people you come across, people you half know.'

'I don't get why you'd be involved at all Chrissie. Adam must have money.'

'Mike, you're so middle class sometimes.'

'Bite me.'

RAY

Naked Woman Holds Up Supermarket With Tin Opener.

It could at a pinch make my list of daily stories to remember, but it would have to be a very weak news day and it would more likely be trounced by a donkey that's learnt to answer the telephone or the member of Mensa who burgled a house but was caught because his muddy footprints led all the way to his home.

Having your truck stolen. Having the last few possessions of value taken from you by violent half-wits wouldn't make the news at all. My last vestiges of status and life are being stripped from me by some greasy disgusting little arse wipe with his arm in a sling, some fruitcake of a woman who either has a drugs problem or is genuinely insane and, the weirdest of all, some accountant sort. The latter is probably the most pathetic of the bunch. He looks like one of those accountants who is so self-conscious that he works in a profession that people feel is dull, that he spends his life maniacally trying to look trendy and youthful. He's the sort who is endlessly intrigued by people who are more free and artistic and just plain out there. They have a romanticised notion that artistic people are somehow more interesting, so they have their noses pressed against the gallery window of life, eyeing up the art.

We are at my house and the little greasy one says he can walk from there and Mike says he's dying for a pee and wants to come in.

We walk into my house and the door has been forced and won't close properly and the place has been turned upside down. There are slashes in the furniture, books all over the floor; in the kitchen there is flour everywhere, where someone has been going through the cupboards and emptying everything out.

I go ballistic. I kick at everything I can find. I pull pictures from the walls and smash them over the furniture. The others stand and look at me. Mike even rights a few items even as I knock over other stuff. I kick and kick and kick at an armchair. I pick up a wooden chair and slam it against the wall, but it doesn't break. I don't break any windows; even in my anger I wonder at this, that they would take long to repair. I calm down. Chrissie is looking for something. She looks at me.

'You got any cigarettes?' she asks.

I find her some cigarettes and we sit together puffing. She still has her tequila which she is getting through like a thing possessed.

'When were you last here?' asks Mike.

I can't remember. Think. Why can't I remember? Maybe two days ago.

'Four days ago,' I reply.

Mike wanders off to the front door. He's looking at the post. The letters, like everything, have been flung around. Mike is looking hard at any envelope he can find.

'I think this happened today. If it had been done yesterday then today's post would just be on the doormat. But it's been scattered with the rest of it. This is postmarked yesterday from London so it seems reasonable it came this morning.'

A regular little Sherlock Holmes.

'Also, by the broken window it looks very dry and I think it rained last night.'

Enough sleuthing already.

I realise I'm feeling better, calmer.

Rick walks in through the front door. I walk straight towards him. I am going to kill him. This is not an empty threat. I am going to break his neck. I am going to pull his head clean off his shoulders. There will be tendons springing from the top of his neck. There will be blood pumping up, hitting the ceiling like a geyser. Red, glaring red blood shooting up from his neck. Torn muscle and a twisted mouth on the head that is pulled away. Rick moves back. He can see the look in my eyes. He almost falls, tripping because I'm moving in on him and he can't get back fast enough.

'Move back,' he says.

I am within two feet of him now. I will kill him. I see him shudder. No, I see him brace himself. I see him cock his head to one side. His eyes half close. He knows he needs to brace himself. He has shot me. I do not hear this or see this. Why didn't I see that he had a gun? He has fallen back and away to one side. He seems to be falling. I know he has shot me. He is dropping the gun. The gun is falling away. I look down at it. It clatters. The barrel is the first to hit the floor. It may fire again as it drops. I watch it drop and then see the red. I see my shoe that is half torn away. I see black and red and flesh. I see the gun hit the ground.

I tear at him. I see part of his arm, it is the first thing in my way and I clench it and tear. I can feel the side of his body. I clench it through his T-shirt and rip. My left hand belts up to hit him in the face. His jaw turns and then his head snaps back. My knee comes up. I will kill him. He tries to punch me but I am in too close and he is falling backwards. His head cracks against the wall. My right hand hits him square and hard. It is my cleanest punch yet and his skin tears by his eye. Rips. There is just a leaf shape of flesh. As he falls away, pin pricks of blood dot the flesh left behind. His head twists and there is blood everywhere now. He is now on the ground and I kick.

Someone is on my back. I turn and sway to remove them, but of course, that won't work. Whoever it is has their hands and arms around my neck. I hit Rick again. I kick him. I am pulled by the weight of the person on my back. I twist and then power back and back. The other wall seems further than I would have thought but I am running now, straight backwards. I lose my balance and fall backwards. I am just far enough back so that as I fall, I slam the person on my back against the wall.

Rick is trying to stand, he is slow to his feet, he sees me running towards him, he tries to move sideways but my hand catches his shoulder and he is down again. I start to kick and kick his stomach.

Mike is shouting. I cannot hear what he is saying. I turn a little. He has picked up the gun. He thinks he can stop me if he picks up the gun. I pull the barrel from his hands. The butt of the gun smacks against him. I smack the butt against him a second time.

Rick stays down. The other two are transfixed. Now I hold the gun. I will kill. I am breathing so hard I cannot think. We wait to see what I will do.

'In the garage you will find strappings.' I say this to Chrissie.

'Strappings?'

'Cloth strappings for the truck. Go and get them and come back within one minute or I will shoot your boyfriend here.'

'Where's the garage?' she asks.

I tell her and she goes. Rick is still down but I haven't killed him. Chrissie returns with some strappings.

'Right Mike. I want you to tie up Rick.'

Ray got me to tie Rick up, and then Chrissie had to tie me up. Finally he tied Chrissie up himself. Ray had taken to scowling at me, from where I'd jumped on his back.

Ray strapped the lot of us up to a bookcase that he had, so we had an uncomfortable time of it, crooked at an awful angle and stuck on a hard floor.

Ray squatted in front of Rick.

'Right,' he said, 'I want to know who organises all this. I want to know names and where to find people. I want to know how to get to them and frighten them and make sure they never trouble me again.'

Rick said he didn't know anything like that. This was very unlikely. Ray stood up and kicked him.

'Let me tell you, you little arsehole. I have nothing better to do for the next day than to kill you slowly.'

He turned to Chrissie, 'And I bet you know a few things, so I won't forget you.'

'Why's he keeping me?' I whispered to Chrissie.

'So you don't run to the police, I guess.'

Ray's foot was a mess and he was wincing when he moved. He took an interest in it out of the blue. He went off and came back with some bandages and a bowl of water.

Ray started trying to peel off his trainer, but parts of his flesh were congealed into the fabric and got pulled as he tried to remove it. The flesh was purple and charred but as far as I could tell the actually damage was much more slight that I first imagined. Basically it was just a mess.

He hobbled off and returned with a knife and some heavy duty looking scissors, and tried to cut away at the shoe.

He started mumbling about this and that as though he were in a daydream.

'You know, it's like as though I'm never allowed anything,' he said. 'When I was married, we got to that stage where we had less and less sex...'

Ray seemed to get stuck.

'You know one year as a Christmas present I bought her some camiknickers. She opened them and look politely at them and then night after night I waited and wondered if she'd wear them and she never did. I asked her once about them and she said, "We don't really go in for that sort of thing, do we?"'

Ray seemed lucid, the effect of what he was saying was madness, but his general air was not.

'What you have to understand is that I didn't even get a stick of furniture. I got nothing,' he said.

'He's a psychopath because his wife didn't want to wear French knickers?' whispered Chrissie.

'Then she had the cheek to knock on the door here. Here! She was just... it was just gloating, seeing me with nothing, seeing me here. She had the cheek to knock on the door. Here.'

Ray was still tending to his foot while he spoke. He continued to run through random grievances from his life and seemed in no hurry to get back to us.

He addressed Rick, 'People have got to see they can't just go treating people like this. You've got to see that. People turn in the end. This is like pay back time, you see?'

Rick looked very bedraggled but didn't look as though he

was going to die.

'I mean, when I think about it, this is the first time I've been in charge of my life for a long time. Ever perhaps,' said Ray.

'Look,' I said, 'Ray, you don't need me and Chrissie.'

'Oh but I do. Chrissie is just the sort who knows everything. She's local. She knows what's what, she's bright, she's outgoing. I should have been someone like you. I moved too much, or I was too ambitious.'

'Can I have a drink or something?' asked Chrissie. 'That tequila must be somewhere. I'm really not feeling well.'

'That habit of yours will be about due to catch up with you,' mumbled Rick.

'Fuck off Rick.'

Ray got as far as he could with his foot and found himself some paper.

'Okay then Rick, tell me who I need to find,' said Ray.

Rick was silent. I noticed his face had stopped bleeding.

'Any chance of that tequila?' asked Chrissie again.

'I'm going to enjoy torturing you Rick. It's every person's dream, isn't it?'

'Oh Jesus,' said Rick.

'Ray, listen,' I said, 'there has got to be some way out of this.'

'I am taking my life back. This is just a piece of scum. He is a leach who takes from everything around him. I have no problem at all with killing him. So Rick, what do you say?'

Chrissie spoke. 'Look before you get carried away, I'm going to need something Ray.'

Chrissie was looking more ill by the minute.

'I've been thinking,' she said, 'either let me go or perhaps if we can get something from the surgery.'

'My surgery?' I asked.

'Well I can't take him home,' she said to Ray, 'My husband

will be there.'

'What are you hoping to get from my surgery?'

'What about that drug you use on patients that makes them whoozy?'

'Hypnovate? I haven't used that for years.'

'Have you got any left?'

'Stock clearing isn't our speciality. Possibly. But don't get me started on the illegalities here, Chrissie.'

'Oh fuck off Mike.'

RAY

I can't resist seeing Mike have to do something illegal, not only is it fun to see Bank Manager Boy go through the agonies of infringing some minor dental law but he would now feel more and more implicated and less likely to shop me.

Although, frankly, Mike is so irritating that if I did away with him it would be no loss. Murder one smuggler, get one petty dentist free.

I check that Chrissie and Rick are secure and I get Mike to drive us to his surgery to pick up the necessary stuff. He isn't unduly brave so I don't have to threaten him too much to make him behave himself.

Back at my house Mike taps up a vein for Chrissie and puts in a small amount. It appears to have no effect so he puts in a lot more. Chrissie had been agitated but she has become disorientated and giggly.

I tie Mike back up.

'I think we're over Chrissie,' mumbles Mike.

It strikes me that Chrissie is too out of it to retain anything said and Mike, the coward, probably knows this.

'I trusted you,' says Mike. 'But you talk your way out of one thing only for another to spring up. It was just one big con that endlessly favours you.'

'Oh moan, moan,' says Chrissie, 'I finally let you into my

life a bit and you just moan at what you find.'

Chrissie stops what she's saying and fixes on Mike in that way a drunk does when they're trying to remember their own thoughts.

'Now listen Mike, you're a tosser, but you're alright. You're alright. You know that? You're alright.'

Mike pretends not to be impressed.

'Look Mike. Michael. Mike,' she says.

She stops for a while, but I like the idea that she is all trussed up and awaiting death and all she can think of is to explain to Mike his faults. This is a couple past first love and indulging in erratic recriminations. I cheerfully wait for more.

'Mike, Mikey, Mike. Do you know when you lost interest in me?'

'I haven't lost interest in you,' says Mike.

'It was when you discovered I wasn't all perfect. All rounded. All sorted.'

'I love you,' says Mike.

'You've got to love me for who I am. You should be happy that things are going well for me. But you just want to possess me and when I'm not the dream person you imagine you make me feel...' she hasn't got hands free any more so she holds her lips open. '...you make me feel that big.'

It is hard to believe that being held hostage and needing to shoot up would be classed as things going well for her.

I turn my attention to Rick. I like the fact that he has been waiting all along for me to get back to him. He is afraid but doesn't want to be seen as afraid. Everything is jogging along nicely.

I get the knife from the table and stab it hard into his shin. It slices down the side of the bone, through the muscle. It gets caught before it has a chance to get through to the other side. I wrestle with it.

Rick gives out a very satisfying scream.

Mike screeches, 'Jesus Christ.'

It is difficult to get the knife back out. It has got caught somehow. I twist it a little and it comes free. Rick is trying kick me and wriggle. A moving target should make it more fun. I stab again but hit the floor. I figure I'll scare him before I even give him a chance to tell me what I need to know.

I put down the knife and grab a foot. I pull at the shoe and Rick tries to thrash his foot around but he is not a match for my strength. Eventually the shoe comes off. I pick up my knife again and I jab sideways with the blade. It catches him this time. Skin rucks up over the blade as it slides forward over his tendons.

I'm having trouble getting Rick's foot to stay still. There are more strappings in the garage. I go off. To make them sweat, I stay away for longer than necessary. When I return I tie up Rick's second ankle so that it can't move. Now I can start stabbing again.

Something is happening to distract me. I think at first it is the other two trying to stop me. I look and Chrissie is moving her legs around. She's still got her supermarket clothes on, but she's trying to work the trousers down. She's managed to get the waist band down to about half way down her thigh.

'Mike,' she say, 'Mike go down on me.'

Scary Girl starts rubbing her legs together.

'This makes you horny?' I ask.

'It's the drug,' says Mike looking a glorious combination of weary and shitless.

Chrissie manages to raise herself up so that she is half standing. She gets one leg over Mike's body and pushes her crotch in his face. Mike's face is framed by the V of her legs. The elasticated waistband of the cheap blue trousers is riding up against his chin.

'Lick me,' she is saying.

Chrissie pushes herself harder against Mike's face.

I turn to Rick, 'While Mike is licking the nice lady, perhaps you can start telling me a few things.'

'Piss off,' he says.

I start to cut his legs open. Methodically this time. I draw my knife sideways across his skin over the shin bone. There are no decent arteries there so I can torture him without killing him. For days if necessary. I draw another line parallel to it about half an inch below. Then a third, then a fourth.

I go off to get some toilet paper to mop up the blood so that I can see what I'm doing more clearly.

I now cut vertical slits in the skin but much deeper. All the way down to the bone this time, in centimetre strips. I want to peel the strips down. I want to cut out every other square like a chess board, then peel down the chequered strips. But how?

I go off to the kitchen and look for a useful implement. I return and start my job. Chrissie is still squirming over Mike's face. I start cutting the squares away and then paring the strips away from the bone.

Rick is pleading but mostly I don't hear him.

'I don't know that much, but there's no way I can tell you what I do know. These people will kill me.'

The bone is almost grey. The flesh pulls away slowly. It's sickening, but I don't want to show that I find it sickening. Thin white strands of tissue hold the flesh to the bone; they stretch and break over and over again as I pull.

'I will kill you,' I assure him. I feel slighted that I am somehow less a threat than whoever employs him, otherwise why won't he tell me things? This is something I can put right with a little time and effort.

I'm getting the hang of this now. I brace the other leg and go for the shin again. But this time I cut it in one large fillet. I slice down vertically pushing the blade hard and flush with the bone. Some of it I have to lever at and twist in order to pull it away, other bits peel cleanly. I have a good rectangular flap now that is about six inches long and about one inch, perhaps two inches, wide. I pull at the flap with my fingers. I am intrigued. It has shrunk, curled. It would no longer fill the gap on the leg left behind.

I pull at the flap with my hand. The top of it stretches and tears, but with effort I can get it onto the floor. I stab the knife into the flesh pinning it to the floor board. It doesn't stick the first time so I stab a second time, harder.

I have a plan to get nails. I will nail Rick's flesh to the floor. Even if I let him go, he will need to get the end of the hammer and lever out the nails. I will hammer the nails in so tight that he will have to crush his own flesh to get the claw of the hammer under the nail.

MIKE

Ray's face was metallic white. Shiny. Rick had beads of sweat as big as rain drops all over his face and arms.

Ray had trouble keeping Rick's legs still so he had tied them up at the ankle and attached them to the table leg. Rick had enough power to move the table so Ray then set about tying the furthest table leg to the radiator.

Ray was gashing at Rick's leg in curled intersecting patterns. He then went off to the kitchen for what felt like forever and came back with a tea spoon.

Rick was pleading for his life. He was coming out with every last detail he could think off; information to buy off Ray. There seemed to be a duel scam going on. The load in the lorry itself was important. They were some kind of rock that they were using to lay beneath the surface of the Reapham bypass, perhaps to sabotage it. It was incomprehensible. But there was also supposed to be something hidden in the cab. It was this item that was missing and was causing all the trouble. The whole thing was financed between Julio Barrio and James Palmos.

But Ray was turning a deaf ear. Rick had left it too late.

Chrissie meanwhile was totally out of it with the drug she was on and spent a minute or so having a go at me, and then another minute trying to squirm all over me.

Then she got transfixed with what Ray was doing with his

teaspoon. He had got the end of it and was levering the flesh up in clumps. He was digging with prods and twists. There were bits of flesh falling on the floor like pieces of bloodied pork skin with bits of hair on it, thin hair about two centimetres long. Other bits of the flesh were falling sideways but remaining attached by tags. Blood everywhere. The only good news from Rick's point of view was that Ray confined himself to attacking only one leg

There was a movement beyond my line of vision. Something out of focus in the corner. Someone picked up the gun. There were two people there. Ray stood up to face them, but he was on the wrong foot. His right foot was caught below Rick's and that was tied up. I could see a skirt and the barrel of the gun being raised.

DAVID

Francis had been hanging around my office gloating.

'I saved you from yourself,' he said.

'How so?'

'Those immigrants took themselves out to the nearest village and picked fights with local lads.'

The security is so lacking at the Immigration Centre that I appeared to be the only person they were successfully stopping from going in and out. Although I'd heard the same from a cub reporter on the Evening News. They seemed to be putting more effort into controlling the press than immigrants.

'If we'd ran a orphan campaign as you'd suggested,' continued my editor, 'we would have looked pretty stupid. And we'd have kissed goodbye to our sales down that way. By the way, are you interested in covering this story?'

'Perhaps it's not the sort of story I do best,' I replied.

'Mmm. Aliens is more your line.'

'I guess,' I said.

Mercifully Julio and Sue turned up. Sue, rather bizarrely, was wearing an evening dress. It was three in the afternoon. She was effervescent with happiness, like sodium buzzing around on water. Julio was only marginally more subdued. Francis, realising he was out of tune with the mood, pissed off.

'Go home!' Sue commanded. 'Get your very best clothes.'

Julio appeared behind her.

'No,' said Julio. 'It's better to be specific. Get clothes you would wear to the opening of an art exhibition.'

I looked nonplussed.

'Now!' said Julio.

I went home and returned half an hour later.

Julio and Sue looked me up and down.

'Second thoughts,' said Julio, 'We're going shopping.'

Something was definitely up. Julio drove me and Sue into Cambridge. We went to the best designer shop the city had to offer. Assistants fussed around me. Sue and Julio fussed around me. I felt like a bride, but I looked like Jimmy Nail. In Prada. Or Nicole Farhi. Or Agnes B or whatever it was they kept trying to get me to wear.

Julio picked up the tab, then took us to a bar 'where he was known.' We were treated like royalty. The avuncular owner busied out and pulled up a chair to talk with us a while.

'So this is David?' he said. I felt very special.

At seven o'clock Sue bobbed up and announced, 'And now for the surprise.'

'It's about five minutes away,' said Julio who was equally excited.

'You see,' said Sue, 'we've been thinking about you. And really you've been depressed for a long time and getting more and more into a rut.'

'No I haven't.'

Sue continued, 'There's that awful awful pig sty you live in. You don't look after yourself.'

'You drink too much,' added Julio.

Thanks Julio.

'You talk about cartooning but you hardly even send your stuff off any more. You get out less and less. You look a permanent mess. I'm not sure you even wash. You don't even have the spirit to get your car repaired. You barely reply to emails any more; I can write three or four and you'll just send a short one in return, or you won't send one at all, and then I wonder if I've offended you and I pluck up courage to come and see you.'

It was about emails.

'I thought you didn't mind that,' I said.

'I don't,' said Sue. She obviously did. 'But let's face it. You're chronically depressed.'

I started to protest. We turned the corner and there was a gallery dead ahead of us, lit up brightly. There were people visible in the windows milling around with wine glasses.

And my name splashed across the windows.

We were greeted at the door by Mad Chrissie's husband, Adam. He's a middle-aged and very likeable promoter.

'David!' he cried. 'Julio came to me with this idea, and when I saw your work... well!'

He turned, sweeping his hand out in a gesture to show me the exhibition they had put on. He sent a glass of wine flying down a woman's front.

I was taken on a tour round.

My cartoons had been mounted or occasionally framed. Sometimes they had captions. A lot of them were of Julio himself. I hardly recognised any of the people there. Presumably the gallery lures in their regulars with vague promises of white wine. It didn't worry me; any person for me to show off to would do.

Julio was standing by a cartoon of himself which he particularly liked. It showed him serving at a trestle table out near the New Age encampment.

It was in five frames, and Julio was offering 'Homeopathic Drinks'. He got some whisky and poured it into a tumbler. He then poured it back into the bottle leaving just a hint of whisky in the glass. He then filled the glass with water to the top, diluting it to the nth degree, then discarded the water and repeated the process. He then sold it to a hippy.

'There you go,' he said, 'homeopathic whisky. £5 please.'

Julio was beside me, wetting himself with happiness.

'They'd fall for it, you know,' he said. 'And think of the mark-up on my whisky!'

The next cartoon was of me at home, making an attempt to clean. There was a board on the wall covered in dried spaghetti, yellowed tea bags and general crud. I scrub and clean at it over several frames and after removing an inch of grime, I discover the board is in fact a window. Through it, I can see a dank misty Fen winter. I look at it solemnly for a frame, and then try to recover it with handfuls of grime to block the view.

There were cartoons of the Polish workers, of Arkwright's shop; you name it, it was there.

There was a television monitor rigged up. it showed the footage of Julio trying to prevent his car from running up hill. When he got to the top of the hill, the footage reversed so that it looked as though he were pushing the car back down again. The footage would then reverse again, and so on.

'I felt we needed to associate you with an image people already knew,' said Adam.

'Absolutely,' I said.

Julio tapped a glass. He called for attention.

'And now for the highlight of the evening,' called Julio. 'The launch of David's book!'

Sue walked in with a pile of books.

My books. Books of my cartoons.

It was the best day of my life.

I leafed through one of the books. I found myself quibbling with which cartoons they chose to highlight, but I didn't say anything.

Adam brought out a huge easel with a sketch pad on it. He handed me a felt marker. Everyone craned to see what I would do.

'You must have tremendous faith in my talents,' I said.

I started to sketch the people in the gallery as a group. Julio beaming, half the size of the others. Adam looking like a fat cat: I made a couple of his wrinkles look like whiskers. I sketched some of the others present but started to panic. Of the thirty or so pictures on show in the gallery, I realised that not one of them had been of Susan.

I looked across at her. She was watching me intently. She looked as apprehensive as I felt.

I couldn't avoid her. I started to sketch her. I started with her body: something I never do as a rule. Instead of showing her short legs and long torso, I put her in a 1920's dropped waist dress and high heels. I hesitated over the face. Not David Coultard, anything but David Coultard. There had to be some other famous square face that wasn't ugly. That slight difference that made Anjelica Huston stunning in one light but not another. My brain was freezing. Anjelica Huston had nothing to do with anything. Think David, think.

Jackie Kennedy.

Jackie Kennedy.

Jackie Kennedy should have been ugly. She had an eye on each corner, for Christ's sake. She had Judy Garland brink-of-madness eyebrows. She had that defeated smile, that rag doll body language. And that was before JFK's death.

I started drawing Jackie K, tweaking the image as I went. People were expecting to see Sue, so they saw Sue. What was my craft, after all, if not to celebrate people?

The picture was complete. People cheered and clapped. I felt like crying with happiness.

'Is that okay?' I asked Sue.

'It's fantastic,' she said. But somehow she didn't look quite right.

'Would you like to keep this?' I asked. 'Or I could do another the same but just of you.'

'I would prefer that,' she said. It was the first time I'd ever seen her beam.

Julio drove us home that night. It was very late and I was chattering away like a child. Julio dropped us off at Sanity Row. I could walk home from Susan's. I hugged Julio in the darkness and thanked him again.

'Well just make sure you're still in at work first thing tomorrow,' he joked. Well, half joked.

We were at the wrong end of Sanity Row, so had to walk about half the length of it.

Sue stopped up short.

'That's Mike's car, and Rick's car,' she said.

'So?' I asked, but she was obviously curious and in my drunken state it was kind of contagious.

The house they were parked outside was brightly lit inside.

Sue, bold as brass, knocked on the door, but there was no answer.

Sue prowled around the outside. She looked through the letterbox and taking her cue I decided to look through the window that was right by, but the curtains were too well closed to see anything.

Sue beckoned me to look through the letterbox with her. It was one of those houses where the door goes straight into the front room and then I realised I could see just about see Rick's head in there, but he was sitting on the floor or something.

There was obviously something really wrong. I don't know what I was thinking, but I realised that the door had been forced at some stage and would open by pushing. Sue just wandered straight in.

The next few seconds were fast and blurred. Sue was slightly ahead of me. I was hanging behind waiting to sound apologetic to whoever owned the place. I saw Rick on the floor and I could see that he was tied up and looked very ill and had a gash on his face. There was glass everywhere. It looked as if someone had been smashing the place up. I turned my head to get a better view of the scene and saw a large man in the sort of clothes they wear at a supermarket deli counter. He lurched towards Sue but then seemed to go backwards. Then he seemed to get taller, and then in that way where you notice the wrong things at the wrong time I saw Scary Chrissie who was also in a supermarket uniform.

Then the man who was standing captured my attention but I didn't know why at first. The side of him fell away. Like a huge semicircular chunk of him disappeared from his waist and he went straight down. There was a massive bang which was louder after it had gone; after my brain had had time to register it.

Sue had shot him. I looked at the gun she was carrying, then the man's head crack back against the wall which he then slithered down. Sue swung slowly to the left. I don't know at what stage I saw Mike, but a bit like a dream, when I saw him I realised I'd known he was there all along.

MIKE

Sue was wearing evening clothes and went straight to the gun and picked it up. She was saying things rapidly and loudly that got lost in the chaos. Ray swung towards her and then she pulled this amazing face, her chin contorted in, her neck pulled sideways, her eyebrows went together, and she fired the gun.

David was behind her. He was half cut and none too steady, so I winced as he came towards me with a knife to cut me free. Chrissie in her disorientated way said she needed a pee, so when she was released she wandered off.

Sue was shaking. Her head was twitching, her eyes were transfixed on Ray. She sat down.

'Sue faints with blood usually,' said Rick.

Sue put her head between her legs.

I was the only person who ran forward to help Ray. He was unconscious but blood was still pouring out of him. I tried to find a pulse in the neck. I held my ear close to his nose to see if he was breathing.

I shouted, 'Call an ambulance.'

But Sue was in shock and Rick appeared not to hear me.

I tried to lug Ray squarely onto his back and pull his jaw forward to give him mouth to mouth. I shouted for an ambulance again and then kept blowing into his lungs, I kept placing three fingers in the bottom of his ribs to find where to massage his heart, then pushing it down an inch, over and over again. I screamed at people to help.

People were milling around but no one was doing the right thing. There was screaming from somewhere.

I stopped, my hands raised as if admitting defeat. I went off to find a phone, but as I started to call, Rick appeared from nowhere and was flustered.

'What are you doing?' he asked.

'I'm calling the ambulance.'

'But he's dead.'

'You still have to call the ambulance, it's the law,' I said, 'we've just committed a murder.'

'Well not really,' he replied.

I put the phone down to discuss it. Chrissie appeared with four mugs of tea.

She looked around. 'Oh I should have made five,' she said. She disappeared again, then almost instantly reappeared with one mug. She put it down then brought back the four mugs she previously had. She bent down to Sue. 'I've put lots of sugar in it,' she said.

Rick took the phone from me and slumped down on the floor. He found a knife from somewhere and cut cleanly through the phone cord. After a pause he spoke slowly.

'Look,' he said, 'if you get the police in, we're going to have to explain away why the trucker would want to kidnap us in the first place.'

'He was a psychopath,' I said.

'No. I mean yes, but why these particular people? We'd have to go into what we were all doing with his truck.'

'I didn't do anything,' I protested.

'We'd have to explain why we shot him in the foot.'

'Look we can think of something,' I said.

'In the five minutes till the coppers come? And then there's

Matt. He's the sort they arrest just to make up the numbers. When they catch up with him, he's so fucking dopey, we can't rely on him.' Rick was fading fast. 'Just think about it,' he said.

We found ourselves sitting in a circle with our mugs of tea and the corpse a couple of feet away. It was a very surreal sight. David in an over-designed suit. Rick with half of one leg missing. Sue in an evening dress.

Rick had found some sheeting at some stage and was now ripping it up and tying it round his leg.

'How are you going to get rid of the body, Rick?' I asked. 'He'll be missed sooner or later. No matter how clever you think you are, you'll leave evidence. At the end of the day it was self defence.'

Sue, the killer, sat there in silence. David just looked dazed.

'It's just attention we don't need,' said Rick. 'The man's dead. It makes no difference what we do now.'

David spoke up. 'But I'm not involved at all.' For no apparent reason, he was fingering a book of cartoons.

There was some noise outside. The pounding of car stereos, the slamming of doors. Cars racing off again.

Chrissie said in an abstract voice, 'The local lads do a lot of joy riding round here.'

Sue leant forward to say something to Rick which none of us caught.

Rick was gripping his thigh, he looked too ill to do anything more.

I took Chrissie by the hand and stood, and without saying a word I led her out. She put an arm out as we moved to gather up the tequila, and we walked out of the house.

'Where are we going?' she asked.

'Home.'

There was a voice behind me. Ricky was up again and

telling me to stop. I set my head determinedly forward, but it was obvious that I just wasn't brave enough so I soon looked back. Rick was framed by the light of the doorway, dashing back as best he could into the house. I took this as my cue to run towards my car. Chrissie, with the Hypnovate still in her veins, was swinging alarmingly on the end of my arm. I was trying to pull Chrissie as fast as she would go. I furiously tried to unlock my car, get both doors open and get it started, but Chrissie was swaying around looking very content and in no hurry to sort herself out.

'Get in the car. Now.'

Chrissie stood and grinned.

'Chrissie now! Now! Get in the car! We have got to go.'

'Why's that then?'

Rick reappeared in the doorway with his gun and told us to stop.

I lunged across the passenger seat and tried to grab Chrissie's arm. I pulled her hard and she fell forward and started complaining.

Rick shot at us and the back window of the car shattered.

'Jesus, Rick,' shouted Chrissie, she sounded disappointed rather than alarmed. 'That's really fucking dangerous.'

I pulled her a second time and her torso and a few of her limbs ended up in the car. I threw the car into gear and Chrissie held more or less on with her door wide open.

There were various cars further along the track where Sanity Row meets the old munitions road. Even the parked cars had their lights on and people were milling about, so rather than be seen I took us in a sweep across the common, shouting at Chrissie to hold on tight and shut her door.

We got home, and I realised to my horror that the syringes and vials that I'd taken from the surgery were still at Ray's house.   Chrissie had amnesia about all that so that I had to explain it to her.

'I'll ring up Sue,' I said to Chrissie. 'She can clear it up.'

'Given that Rick tried to shoot you, I don't think he's going to want to help you by removing the evidence that implicates you,' said Chrissie.

'Yeah, but she works for me,' I said. It sounded very lame.

'I do remember some things,' she said. 'I remember the truck and the supermarket and Ray tying us up, but after that...'

I explained a few more details and the fact that it was a pest that she wouldn't be able to back up any story I came up with.

She said, 'If they've got a body to get rid of, then they're hardly going to prioritise a syringe with your fingerprints all over it.   But in the long run it will be a bargaining chip if they want to stop you talking to the police.'

'And that's another thing,' I said, 'we have got to tell the police otherwise we're as culpable as everyone else.'

'Yeah, but you'll get done for drugs running.'

'No I won't.'

'Who drove the car?' she asked.

'You have to have drugs in your car for it to be drugs running.'

'But they'll try and implicate you somehow. Why would Ray have tied you up if you weren't involved?'

'But I wasn't involved.' I was looking ratty.

'At least sleep on it.'

'I can't ring them up tomorrow and say, "Oh yesterday I saw a murder: I thought I'd have a kip before I reported it."'

'People are often slow to report crimes.   The police see it all the time.   Look the man's already dead.'

'I'm not listening to this crap, Chrissie.'   I was shouting.

'Think about it Mike, if you do drugs running, you get struck off and you can't practice dentistry anymore.'

'For the umpteenth time, I didn't do drugs running. I gave you a lift.'

Chrissie was looking alarmed. 'Look forget Matt and Rick, we're talking serious heavy shit people. We're talking people who make you disappear in the night. People you just don't mess with. That is why you should walk away.'

'Yeah Chrissie. I think that's why we have a police force in this country.'

'They will shoot you before you get to be a witness in court. You will disappear. I will wonder for a few days where you went and then find someone else to share a bit of my life with. Perhaps someone younger. And richer.'

I smiled at that. Chrissie smiled, probably pleased to have softened me.

'Chrissie. Listen to me. This is the stuff of myths. We go to the police, they sift through the evidence and they prosecute only when they think they have a good case, which will let us out.'

Chrissie looked as though she were giving up on me.

'Mike you don't know anything about anything. You're an outsider. All you know is who starred in the 1948 remake of Gaslight, and how to stick holes in teeth; it does not arm you for a life in crime. There is some really serious crap in all of this.'

'Yeah, I'm sure. But surely people like that get half their strength from people fearing them and not even questioning whether it's justified. It's all local rumour and then having the right menacing attitude.'

'Does it for me mate.'

'And anyway, the remake of Gaslight was in 1944 not 1948.'

Chrissie took an interest in my cuts and bruises. She got some warm water in a bowl and cleaned up my face and ear. She was very mummsy, very loving, but I was irritable.

Chrissie left the house and I dozed on the sofa, then to my

surprise she returned. She had changed into some decent clothes. She said 'Hi,' cheerfully, but I just nodded in a stoney way. I was angry.

We went up to bed. We curled up naked in spoons. Chrissie turned her head back to me and said, 'Kiss me.'

I still had the air of someone with a grievance. I didn't move towards her.

'Kiss me,' she said again. 'Put your lips over mine. Fuck me.'

I still didn't soften. I kissed her though. I sealed my lips against hers and kissed her for a long time. I took a handful of her hair at the back of her head and pulled it hard. I kept pulling it so that her head was cricked back.

I drew my mouth away and she gasped a deep breath in, then the moment she let it out again I sealed my lips to hers. I made sure that as I breathed there was no movement of air from my mouth to hers. I started fucking her. I pushed and pulled her head. Her fragile body was twisting against mine, writhing. I pressed my face harder against hers. Her head started twisting from left to right, struggling to get air. I fucked her harder and faster, grinding deep inside her. Her chest was heaving ineffectually against mine, her head moving faster now trying to escape, but I went on and on. In flashes I could see the colour of her face, blues and purples. Her struggles got more violent, her hands pulling at my head, sometimes hitting my naked back. Then she slipped away. She relaxed, her limbs falling away from me. Her eyes were closed. Her face was at peace.

DAVID

Nothing in life prepares you for this.

Sue was still split up from Rick, but presumably from years together, turned to him for support and decision making.

But there was the stupidity of it. They'd just shot one person: you don't draw attention to it by going outside and taking a potshot at Mike, inviting the neighbours to ring the police.

When Rick realised that Mike was out of range he sat down defeated. He can't have had much blood left in him, so he was doing pretty well. 'We are so screwed,' he said in a daze. 'I should have run after them. I should have kept them until we'd got rid of the evidence. Because they could be ringing the police now. We should have kept them until we'd sorted everything out and it was their word against ours. We're so screwed.'

'I don't get it,' I said. 'This man was holding you hostage for some reason and you shot him out of self-defence. Why don't you just call the police?'

This made Sue think. 'Yeah, what the hell were you doing here Rick?'

'Oh he was just a mad man,' said Rick.

'Yeah but Mike and Mad Chrissie?' she asked. 'And the butcher's clothes. And your legs. What the hell have you all been up to?'

'It's better you don't know,' he said.

'Better for you, you mean,' she said.

'You're the one who killed him,' he said.

As he said that, we were more aware again of the body on the floor.

'What were Mike and Mad Chrissie doing here?' I asked no one in particular. They were a weird enough pairing at the best of times. Chrissie, the distraught neurotic. A woman who thought she had tinnitus in both ears until she discovered it was just the constant sound of men simpering. When I draw her I go for a painful Ally McBeal body with a hint of dirt here and there. I pencil a little rough patch at the top of her buttock cleavage where her G-string chaffs. No one could possibly get the joke from the cartoon alone, but I put it there anyway. I always draw her cheekbones like organ stops and a frightened look in her eyes. I doubted that she would ring the police, but what about honest Mike?

'Perhaps if I ring him up and ask him not to,' said Sue.

'I'm sorry,' I said, 'I just don't get it. Sue, you shot him in self-defence. You've got nothing to be afraid of. It's not as though it's your weapon. He was holding the other three hostage for some reason and...'

'It's Rick's weapon,' said Sue. 'Why would he be wandering into a house with his own gun?'

'But they don't know it's his gun.'

Rick said, 'Idiot Matt might well tell them if questioned.'

'So what is the truth Rick?' asked Sue.

'We should get out of here,' said Rick, 'It'll give us a chance to sort out our stories. If we're asked we'll say we panicked. No, we'll say the phone was cut and we went off to look for a phone.'

'But we're leaving fingerprints behind,' said Sue. 'We won't have time to wash every last wall and tea cup or whatever, and they only need the slightest bit of evidence.'

'We'll get rid of the body then,' said Rick. 'No body and they'll think Mad Chrissie's been hallucinating.'

I stood rooted. Our conversation was making less and less sense. I was so hopelessly confused by what must have happened, and I was still drunk from my evening at the gallery. I had absolutely no idea what we should be doing.

'We must have at least ten minutes till the police come. Twenty if they get stuck behind a tractor.'

'Stuck behind a tractor?' I was incredulous. 'You're getting done for murder or kidnapping or whatever you've been up to, and your best chance is that the police might get caught behind a tractor at midnight?'

'We'll get rid of the body and hope for the best,' said Rick. 'Look Sue, you're the one who did the murder. I don't know why you're arguing with me.'

'You're the one they'll kill,' said Sue.

The situation was getting beyond any reasonable person's comprehension.

'Who's going to kill Rick exactly?' I asked.

Neither answered me.

I think looking back, this sense of not understanding the whole picture was what pushed me in favour of helping rather than going home and ringing 999. Or perhaps it was the fact that everything was happening so fast and was so far outside any normal experience. And, yes, I probably had some misguided loyalty to Sue and yes there seems to be an instinct to go along with what everyone else is doing.

'Sue,' said Rick, 'drive my car to the side of the house. David see if you can drag the body.'

I tried to drag the body but I'm not very strong and there was a flap of flesh that got snagged on the edge of a floorboard or a nail that was protruding a bit, and it pulled and stretched. I didn't hear a tear, but I realised some of it had got left behind and that seemed to encourage a kind of sliming phenomenon where a thick tar-like substance was smeared along. It was a dark purple browny mince where human flesh had been pulverised into a slime. I could feel my stomach rising and my mouth filling up with spit.

Rick had a go and even in the state he was in he seemed to be doing better on his own, but then I'm not very strong. Sue came back and then went into the kitchen wondering where the bin sacks were kept and checking in draws. She announced that she would line the boot of the car to stop blood getting in the fabric.

I realised I was in a bit of a daze and I worried that I'd kind of frozen up, like in some bad dream where you're desperate to do something but somehow you never get round to it.

Sue had the boot of Rick's car open and I took all the tools out from there and stuck them on his back seat. Sue lined the back with bin sacks.

'Can someone open a door,' called Rick.

I opened the door and before we knew it, the body was outside. We heaved the body up into the boot of the car.

We kept looking out for car lights but there was nothing. I was thinking that despite all the verbiage and panic, this had only taken us maybe a few minutes so far and we might be alright for time, but when you're panicking or drunk, it's hard to tell.

We dropped the body onto the ground and unwrapped it and heaved it in. It pushed half the bin sacks away, which spoiled the point of them and Sue was all for rearranging them which was a mad waste of time. Rick was straining away trying to get the head to fold in.

'Mind the speaker,' said Ricky.

Ray's boot was pushing hard against some speaker cables. It

wasn't as though it was Ray's fault, but in a funny way, Rick was addressing the body as he spoke.

We put the rug over the top and Rick drove off.

I don't remember us deciding that he'd go on his own, but I suppose that whereas it just about made sense that I'd help lug the body to the car, it wouldn't be my place to help bury the body. Nor would I want to.

With Ricky gone it was suddenly as though I'd dreamt the whole thing. I was left with Sue, just as I had been before we walked into the house.

Sue suggested we leave the back door open and if we heard anything we'd run straight off into the darkness. But she thought if we got rid of the very worse evidence it would help our case. See if anyone's clothing was there, perhaps.

The blood and guts in the front room were grouped mostly in a small area but there were specks and streaks all over the place. There was also glass here and there but we didn't know why. I knew we only had a few seconds or a minute or so, so I tried to think what best to do. We got it into our heads that if we could at least get rid of the worst of it then an outsider would at least not take one look and think, 'My God a murder's gone on here.'

I rushed around the kitchen like an idiot looking for some rubber gloves and a cloth and stuff. All I could find to clean with was Ajax cream which I don't like using and I filled the washing up bowl with water and washing up liquid, and took a cloth and the Ajax into the front room.

My every other thought was that I was doing totally the wrong thing and that aiding and abetting would land me in jail. But these thoughts were repeatedly overridden by the fact that everything was so gross and that I'd made a decision and was hopelessly short of time: too short of time to keep changing tack. I didn't have any gloves and there were bits of flesh and what looked like liver smeared around. I tried to gather it up in the cloth but there was too much for the one cloth. I found a newspaper and I tore bits off and used those to pick up bits and pieces, and then I started cleaning but at first the blood just swirled around on the floorboards.

At no particular point I took the bowl into the kitchen and poured it down the sink. I knew it was time to run.

To my horror, the sink refused to drain. It just filled up with a tawny soup with bits of torn newspaper and flesh.

I was transfixed for a few seconds willing the water line to down, but it was exactly an inch from the top and wasn't going anywhere. I thought perhaps there was a plug in the bottom but I couldn't see through the water. I braced myself for what seemed like an eternity and pushed my hand down into the water. Shudders ran the length of my body as I delved around. No plug, but perhaps too much flesh and paper in the plughole. I tried to stir it with my finger. No joy.

I thought that if I got some bleach it might kind of dissolve things a bit or stop them identifying it or something. I hadn't had much experience of cleaning, so basically I didn't know anything.

I couldn't see the bleach on the kitchen table and then I thought I might have put it back, so I hunted in the cupboards and then I thought that I'd got it all wrong and that I'd only found Ajax, not bleach, and then I panicked again about the time.

I found two sink plungers of different sizes under the sink: it was clear that Ray was used to having trouble with his drains. I started ramming a plunger up and down in the water, creating a flurry as bits of flesh came up to the surface of the water and swam around. There was very little sign it was working.

Sue had been haring around doing similar things then announced it was time to go, making the decision for us. She rushed back into the front room to find her handbag and by the time she was back, the sink was beginning to drain slightly.

I pumped some more in the sink, but this made the water choppy and it was hard to see if I was helping the water level at all.

I tried to kill some time by rushing round the sitting room again looking for things to do. Back at the sink it was almost clear apart from four or five bits of soggy paper and one bit of human flesh about two inches long and half a centimetre wide that was going a funny grey colour.

God help me, I picked it up in my fingers and fled out the back door.

We ran hell for leather the back way to Sue's place. I'd remembered my book of cartoons, so I had those in one hand and the human flesh in the other. I figured I couldn't just fling it any old place.

We locked the door of Sue's house, as though this would somehow keep all trouble out. I was standing there in a daze and the cat came up and wanted a bit of attention, brushing against my leg forwards and back.

The trouble was, as I leant down to stroke the cat, it spotted the bit of flesh that I was holding and grabbed it out of my fingers and started trying to hurriedly eat it in sort of snatching movements on the floor. It knew it was so delicious that it had to eat it quickly because in its experience anything that lovely was illicit and an irate human was going to be coming after it. I started trying to tug the meat back off Pugsley, and Pugsley started growling at me and clenching it in his teeth more. Then somehow it slipped out of my fingers and Pugsley went tearing off out the cat flap in a flurry of guilt and defiance. So I went running out, but of course Sue had been busy locking the door and it took me twice as long to get out as it did the cat.

Once outside I couldn't find Pugsley and I started to worry

that maybe it would have trouble with the flesh, like when they try to eat a bird whole but end up throwing it all back up again. So I got it into my head that somewhere out there in the dark was a bit of Ray's flesh that would get us sent down for good.

We didn't see Rick again that night so I assumed he was burying the body. Sue was going pretty strange on me. I wanted to go to bed. But she wanted to wash and scrub. She wanted all the clothing put in the washing machine that instant. She had some Lady MacBeth thing going on and she wanted to subject my new Armani clothes to it.

'I haven't got anything to change into,' I said. 'Can't I just sleep?'

Sue went off to see if she could find anything of Rick's that he'd left behind. She wandered back with one of those all-in-one overalls that garage mechanics wear over their clothes. It was covered in grease and grime.

'Come on,' she said, 'I'm not letting you sleep until everything's in the wash.'

I fell asleep on the settee with the washing machine churning away somewhere in the background.

MIKE

In the morning I was pottering around the kitchen getting ready for work.

Chrissie appeared in the doorway. She was naked apart from a jumper she'd borrowed from me. She looked sensational. I ignored her. My bowed head smacked of guilt.

'Hey look, I'm sorry I threw up in your bed,' she said.

I kept doing what I was doing.

'You know, I don't think it was drugs at all. I think they were moving something very precious,' said Chrissie, 'Otherwise they wouldn't be so fussed.' She started making some ground coffee.

'Are you for real?' I asked, my tone was more guilty than aggressive.

'No, I mean, something like precious stones,' she said, 'It can be a VAT fraud, or customs or whatever. Or money laundering. Most money laundering is inefficient: you lose money doing it. If you wanted to move a large sum of money from one country to another and make money while doing it, then diamonds are your thing, or good quality jewellery. It's small, it can't be sniffed out, it doesn't leave traces on your fingers. Plus there's places like Sierra Leone that have trade embargoes and they have to sell their new diamonds cheap on the black market. You have to buy the stones down there, which mops up skipfuls of drug money in one hit, then you have to get the diamonds up to Europe to get them certificated, otherwise they're worth far less.'

I was obviously staring at her.

'You don't believe me, do you?'

I sighed irritably.

'Do you not believe such things happen?'

'Oh I believe such things happen,' I said. I kept up the general air of impatience.

'You just don't believe that someone you would actually meet would be involved,' she said. 'But then you haven't met him. I do know some things, Mike. I'm not stupid.'

I looked bemused at her change of tack.

'Really,' she continued, 'the only downside is that you can't trust anyone, so you want someone keeping an eye on the courier, which is what Rick was doing.'

'If they're that valuable,' I argued despite myself, 'why not carry them yourself?'

'No matter how much they're worth, a lot of professional criminals are not going to risk prison.'

I changed tack. 'Chrissie, listen, I'm going to have to go to the police about all this.'

Chrissie looked very rattled. 'They'll threaten to kill my mother.'

'You're making this up.'

'They have. They have threatened to kill my mother if we go to the police. That is why we didn't report it. Anyway, they've probably buried the body by now.'

There was a knock on the door. I heard Chrissie talking for a while and then two policemen came in, a man and a woman. The woman seemed to be in charge; the man stood in attendance. I could feel the colour drain from my face.

Chrissie said, 'You'll have to excuse Mike a bit, he's not

been well.'

'I'm sorry to disturb you at this time,' said the WPC, 'but a crime has been reported and your car was seen at the right place and time.'

'Oh,' I said.

The WPC smiled. I tried to smile back.

'It has to be said that you,' she said, 'both of you actually, match the descriptions of two of the people involved.'

'What exactly is the crime?' asked Chrissie.

'Robbery.'

'I think I'd remember if I'd committed a robbery, officer,' replied Chrissie.

'I'm sure you would. Especially if you were naked at the time.'

'Can I get changed first?' asked Chrissie.

In the back of the police car, Chrissie took to whispering furiously in my ear. She was concerned that we'd need to have an apparent motive to make our actions credible.

'Does it matter?' I asked my face blackening.

'You've got to come up with a story that makes sense. A story that sounds like a story.'

'We could say it was a bet,' I said.

'A dentist wouldn't commit a crime on a bet.'

'Okay. A stag night that went wrong and we woke up with our clothes stolen.'

'Whose stag night?' she whispered back.

I kept looking nervously at the back of the police's heads to see if they could hear.

'We can't say that; we'd have to come up with witnesses,' I said.

Chrissie went quiet. The police station was in view now. We waited in traffic to turn left and into it.

'Oh Jesus wept, I don't know. Okay. Okay. Okay.' For the first time she looked rattled. 'We were fucking in the countryside and some little kid stole our clothes and you didn't realise I'd shop lifted.'

'Actually that's quite good. Was there anyone else in the car?' I asked.

'No.'

'Where did we fuck?'

'A bit down from the truck. No. In a field near the traffic, near the supermarket. Birthday treat for me.'

'It's your birthday?'

'Yeah,' she said.

We smiled at the officers who kindly opened the car door for us.

We were left in a corridor together for a long time, so our planning in the car suddenly looked over hasty.

I had always felt confident in police stations. I have 'Middle Class Professional' tattooed invisibly on my forehead. Several of the local police are our patients, and while I have seen drunks helped on their way to the cells a little too forcefully, or sobbing women from one of the estates left for hours unattended, I have always been treated courteously and efficiently. My biggest concern was that either I wouldn't know any of the police on duty or that with my cuts and bruises I now looked exactly like the sort of person who did indeed get involved in minor crime.

Chrissie was showing another side of herself. When faced with a gun, I had seen her virtually picking her nails and taking an interest in the countryside, but here she looked alarmingly rattled.

We sat waiting.

'You got previous or something?' I asked.

'No.'

We gazed into space.

'Well a few teenage things,' she said, 'but you know.'

'Sort of,' I said.

A WPC came out of a door and towards us. She almost talked to us, but thought of something and went back. She stood in the doorway to her office talking to someone we couldn't see.

There was something about the way we had to wait again that changed the chemistry between Chrissie and me. We waited and waited.

'Look Chrissie, I might just have to tell the truth in there.'

Chrissie nodded as if she were expecting me to say this. She'd done the best she could.

The policewoman beckoned to me.

'Can we talk to you first please,' she said.

I was ushered into a room that was bare apart from an Army recruitment poster and a smaller card about the Samaritans. I waited for a long time and two PCs came in, both male, with a tape recorder and various pads and files. They had a file on this already.

I said to one of the PCs, 'Don't I know you?'

He replied, 'No.'

'Now so that you don't waste your time and our time denying everything, I'm going to lay out the facts for you,' he said.

I looked at the desk for a while.

'Okay,' I said, 'what do you want to know?'

DAVID

The next morning I woke to find Sue getting together lots of cleaning stuff and a bucket.

'I'm going back up there,' she said.

I looked at my watch. Nine o'clock.

'Is that wise. Going back?' I said. 'Isn't it incriminating if the police find you there?'

'What, they might be staking out the place or something?' she said.

'I don't know.' And of course I didn't know. It turned out this was the exact same time that Mike and Chrissie were down the police station.

Sue gave this some thought and then went off and changed into her dental uniform.

'I'll just pretend I'm walking to work and have a look at Ray's and see what's going on.'

'Are you going to work today?' I asked.

'Hell no. I might meet Mike there. I wonder if I can get one of the girls to drop my pay by though,' she said. 'I could text Emma, I suppose.'

Sue set off in her dental uniform and about ten minutes later returned.

'It looks fine,' she said. She changed again. 'Are you coming?' she asked when she returned.

We walked the length of Sanity Row. There was absolutely no one around, but with every single step I felt the most self-conscious I've ever felt in my life. Somewhere, unseen, a hundred people were watching me.

I felt like some terrible intruder going in the back door, although everything was exactly the way we'd left it. But it was just too quiet. If you were at home cleaning then you would have the radio or telly on in the background to keep you company but Sue and I proceeded in silence.

We also did it largely without the lights on. It was totally stupid. I mean, if you see a light on in a house, or the radio playing out a window, you don't think, 'Oh isn't that suspicious, I'd better go and knock on the door to see what's going on, probably a murder.'

So anyway, the place soon looked a lot cleaner and once we got into the cleaning I stopped being quite so frightened. Note, I do indeed know how to clean. I'm just bloody lazy.

We still instinctively thought Mike would report the murder so we had this constant fear that someone would come, but I didn't think Mike would land me in it badly, because I'd done nothing, except misguidedly help Sue.

I worked at the floor and the wall behind where Ray been shot. I managed to find baked beans stuck on a plate at one stage and I wasn't sure if they were important, so I cleared them up anyway. There was lining paper on the wall and the blood and stuff had soaked into it slightly. I didn't have a scouring pad but in the kitchen I found a Brillo. I ended up with a wear patch on the wall where the paper got a bit soaked and rubbed away. I figured no one ever went to prison on the basis of a scrubbed patch on the wall.

There were strange strappings tied round the legs of furniture and fastened to the radiator, which took a lot of shifting. But generally we were pleased at how quickly the room looked better, and the perfectionist in me wanted to put the furniture and books right. So of course the moment I put one bit of furniture right, the next bit looked shoddy and so I spent far more time than I thought. I stood back and admired it. It looked good. You really wouldn't know anything had happened.

Then I saw the sofa. One of the cushion covers had blood on it. Sue and I stared at it for a while. Out of the blue I felt a kind of shock, I felt ill. I had felt funny walking back into the house, but more in a nervous way; now, with the sofa thing I felt ill for the first time. It made no sense.

There was a knock from somewhere. It was the back door. We stood rooted. Then my legs wanted to go. There was a knock again, but this time I didn't know where it was. We could say we were cleaners, but they'd take our details anyway. No, they'd just arrest us. Then I realised it was the back door. The back door must be better. The back door was opening.

'Oh Rick, Jesus wept, you terrified me,' said Sue. 'Why didn't you just let yourself in?'

'It was a bit stuck. I thought you'd locked it.'

Rick didn't look around. He wasn't grateful for the work we'd done.

He said, 'Look we've got a problem,' and then he didn't say anything which, given how fraught everything was, was the worst possible thing he could have said; he just kept looking around.

'Come on then spit it out,' said Sue.

Still he didn't reply.

I said, 'Look we've got a problem with this cushion cover.' When I looked at it again I felt whoozy, but less so this time. I realised the whole phenomenon could have been a hangover.

'Well just turn it over,' he said.

'You thick or something?' I said. It was very out of character.

'How about dry cleaning it?' said Rick.

'Yeah,' said Sue, 'but the dry cleaners might remember dry cleaning a cushion cover, and we'd have to carry it round in the car and then we'd have to get it back again.'

'We could burn it,' said Rick.

'What, now? Everyone will see.' I was warming to standing up to Rick.

'What's your problem?' asked Sue.

'What do you mean what's my problem?' Rick looked puzzled.

'You said you had a problem.'

'Oh, yeah. We've got to get rid of the body. I mean I'm having trouble getting rid of the body.'

MIKE

The police questioned, and listened, and questioned some more. They asked me again and again what I must have thought sitting naked in the car.

'Surely sitting in a car that close to the supermarket, you would have seen what was going on.'

'No.'

'And what about the other people in the car?'

'What other people?'

'We have eye witnesses that there were other people in the car. Do you mean to tell us that none of them knew what Miss Hedges was up to?' When he says the word 'Miss' his lips seemed in close up to me.

'There was no one else in the car,' I said.

They seemed to quite like the case. No one was breaking into a sweat.

'When you were given the supermarket uniforms, you must have realised she hadn't paid for them. You can't go into the supermarket and buy the staff uniforms.'

'I thought they'd just been kind or something. I mean she was naked. A female member of staff would relate to that and be helpful.'

'Tell me,' said the younger PC who was looking very pleased with himself. 'Why would she have asked for four sets of clothing, if there were only two of you?'

'Did she ask for four?' I replied.

'You know she did. You know sir, you're losing all pretence of even trying to be straight with us.'

I said, 'Perhaps Chrissie was worried about sizes, so she wanted a range of outfits to try on. You know how women like to get clothes right.' The two PCs had had enough. They sighed loudly for my benefit. I was asked to wait outside and Chrissie was taken in.

I sat on my own for an eternity.

Finally Chrissie appeared.

'We're going home apparently,' she said. She was trying not to smile.

'Home,' I said. 'My home.'

DAVID

'Digging? Oh Christ Rick, where's the body?' This was Sue.

'In the back of the car.'

'It's still in the back of the car?'

'I thought I'd be able to do it, but I'm just too ill.'

I have no explanation to offer for what I did. What is certain is that somehow I agreed that I was going to help them that evening, bury a body in the fens.

I went home and got changed, then showed my face at the office.

Julio was there. Face like thunder.

No he just had a hangover.

He said, 'Midday, David. The amount you drank I'm surprised you managed to turn up at all.'

The worrying thing was I didn't remember drinking much at all.

'It's been...' I began. 'Hey thanks for the clothes. And the book. Wow. How did you get it published?'

'Let's just say, I've got a bit of an interest in a publishers,' he said.

'Fantastic,' I said.

'Ah, the least you deserve.'

Julio had about four half-brained ideas for stories he wanted me to print. They all blatantly promoted businesses of his. Fine by me.

'Tell me,' I said. 'How did you manage to fake that uphill phenomenon?'

Bad move. Julio's face went grey with indignation. I was convinced he was going to erupt, but he checked himself.

'Why don't you just learn to do your job, David?' he said and walked out.

We were driving along in Rick's car. It was very dark. Sue was moaning and worrying.

'What if we get stopped?' she kept asking.

'Why would we get stopped?' asked Rick.

'I don't know. If one of our headlamps doesn't work, or we've got no tax disc.'

'We've got a tax disc.'

'You know what I mean.'

It was the longest, slowest drive ever. It even turned out that Rick had no plan where we were going. He told us he'd tried to dig a hole to get rid of the body in the middle of nowhere, only for a car to come by. He probably hadn't been seen, but he figured that if the body was ever found then whoever was in the car might come forward. It was all 'what ifs' but it made a kind of sense.

So we did this tour of the Fens in the dark looking for somewhere we could take the car where no one else would go and the farmer or whoever owned the place wouldn't be able to see.

Sue insisted we drove at exactly thirty miles an hour so that we wouldn't get stopped for speeding at least, and Ricky took the view that we'd look suspicious going at the speed limit.

Sue replied that he's always full of some stupid reason why he should drive too fast so they argued about it. Neither was going to give ground so they started shouting.

They calmed down a bit and ended up going at exactly thirty-five but the moment the arrow flickered even a fraction above, they'd start all over again. Rick was spending far too much time looking at the dial instead of the unlit road, but I didn't want to add my grouses to the equation, so I kept quiet.

We went out beyond Isleham way on the back road that takes you off towards the American Air Force bases. We found some ploughed land and we drove towards a field a bit. It was blacker than black so we had to leave the headlights on.

Rick had two shovels which had some bits of concrete stuck to them, and there was a fork that was smaller than normal that looked antique and quite frail but it must have been used for gardening one way or another. Sue took this to be hers.

Ricky got some of the bin sacks from the boot and tucked it round the number plates so that we couldn't be reported easily. Then we got on with the digging.

Sue had all the wrong clothes on and was moaning about her shoes and although the soil was easy to dig, it was also quite waterlogged, so by the time we were a foot down we were just working in a glorified puddle: we were taking sludge out from the bottom and apparently making little headway. After a while Sue lost heart and went to sit in the car.

This caused another row with Rick. He split his time between haranguing Sue through the car door and getting on with the job.

Sue then got out of the car all the better to harangue Rick back. Apparently Rick hadn't praised her enough for cleaning up Ray's house.

'But you were the one who did the murder, you dopey cow,' he said.

'Yeah but it only happened because you were involved in one of your stupid schemes. And besides, we wouldn't have to cover it up if it wasn't for that. I could have just gone to the police.'

I stayed out of it and kept digging.

None of us noticed at first, therefore, when a car appeared in the distance.

Rick stabbed the spade into the ground and we ran to the car. Rick turned off the headlights. We shut the doors and lay there in the darkness. My head was squashed close to Rick's but I was determined not to touch him.

We lay there for what felt like a year but eventually the lights got brighter and flicked in lines across the ceiling above our heads. The car went past without slowing. Rick got out and started digging again.

When it finally came to burying the body we were all dreading even touching it. We'd left the body a long time by then and when we'd first killed him it was like a live person who was unconscious, but now it was a corpse which was far worse. I couldn't bring myself to even prod it, let alone pull it against me and carry it.

Rick eventually had a go and he pulled at an arm. Then he went to the other side and pulled at a leg.

'I think it's stuck,' he said, stating the obvious. We both pulled together, but with less effort as though to justify to ourselves that we had a problem.

'He's got rigor mortis or something,' he said. 'We stuffed him in but now he's frozen where we put him and he's too spread out to get back out the door.' He thought for a while. 'We'll have to cut his legs off or something. We'll have to go back and get some saws and cut his legs off or his head.'

'We can't drive all the way back, Ricky,' said Sue. 'I mean, we might not even find this spot again. We could be driving around all night or we might have to dig another hole.'

'We? I don't remember you doing much digging.'

'Oh don't start, you two,' I said.

'I might be able to chop his leg off with a spade,' said Rick. He went off and came back with the spade. He tried to push it down the side of Ray and use it like a crowbar. He tried the other end of the body and it gave a bit, but it didn't really work.

Then for no reason he started hitting the body with the spade.

'Rick!' I shouted.

He didn't hear me. He just kept belting it. It made no sense whatever. The body didn't seem to be affected at first, but he just kept slamming his shovel into it, and then you could see where some of the clothing was torn and then the side of the body looked what can only be described as kind of dented and gashed. There was no blood.

Sue was screaming by now and Rick turned his head in slow motion towards me. It was as if he didn't know who we were or where he was. I thought he was going to attack me.

Sue kept pleading with him to stop, but he had already stopped. She was crying.

I said, 'Look, if we get back in the car, can we not push the body through? With our feet or something?'

'The seats don't fold down,' said Sue.

Eventually Sue had a good idea and was so pleased with herself and that it would be one up on Ricky that she'd thought of it.

'Have you got a tow rope?' she asked.

Sue knew he had a tow rope because he was a mechanic but she wanted him to answer. He didn't. Sue wanted to spin it out.

'Rick? Have you got a tow rope?'

I went to look in the back seats, where I'd put all the stuff earlier and sure enough there was a chain for towing vehicles.

We got the chain and spent half an age feeding it down over the body. Touching the body hadn't got any easier but I was desperate for this to work.

We looped the chain and then drove the car back until it was right up against a tree and then passed the chain round that. Rick then got in and drove the car forward.

The car moved about four inches and then simply stalled. Rick turned the key again, revved up and then slowly let the clutch back in but the car just seemed to shake in little forwards and backwards motions. Ricky stopped and got out.

As far as we could work out, the system was good enough but the weight of the body got the chain pushed down hard against the edge of the boot and it was getting snagged. There was also the chance that the car was grinding its way down into the mud, which really couldn't be good.

'Perhaps we could attach the chain further up the tree?' I suggested.

'It won't go that much higher because we haven't got that much extra length,' said Rick.

'It's worth a go.'

'We can't keep getting it wrong because the car will get more and more stuck in the mud,' replied Rick.

I said, 'Perhaps if we lift the chain up as we drive it away, so it doesn't get caught.'

'But then the moment it gets tight the chain will pull straight and catch again, or trap our fingers.'

We went one better. Rick suggested I drove, because Sue was new to driving, and clutch control wasn't her forte. I got in the driver's seat while Ricky and Sue stood behind and pulled the body itself up, so that the chain was clear.

I revved up the car as fast as I dared and then slowly let the clutch down bit by bit. I found myself wincing waiting for it to engage. Nothing happened for an eternity, and Rick started calling from the back that he couldn't hold the body up forever. I let the clutch out more and more, or so it felt, and then I think I lost patience because I must have gone an inch too far and too soon and I went shooting forward. There was a heave and the car jerked and snagged, then there was a release as I went shooting into the darkness. I didn't think to put my foot on the brake for a few seconds so I got a worryingly long way. Then the car fell down into the field.

I walked back through the darkness to find Rick and Sue. It was so dark out there, but as far as I could make out they were both pulling themselves out from where they'd fallen underneath the body. The body was out of the boot, but they didn't seem very pleased.

MIKE

I went with the usual suspects to see a film; it was a teen slasher movie of sorts. As we filed out of the cinema one of us mumbled that it was a lean week for film.

We had a meal out.

'Didn't this used to be a noodle bar?' I asked as we sat.

'Last time we were in here, it was,' said Gabby.

I was gleefully telling them the story of holding the supermarket up and our arrest. But in this telling Chrissie forgot to drop the cat and rushed into the car with it. We sped around the supermarket car park and the cat was hurling itself against the windows. Because we were still naked we got scratched to hell, but we finally let it out a few miles down the road and, in this version, Chrissie was wandering around in the dark trying to show it the food she'd got it. Gabby complained that the story was wrong and that she'd heard that Chrissie had been all for keeping the cat and still had it living with her.

'Ya dee ya,' I replied and we got talking about other things.

Alan had been quiet all evening but he took a lull in the conversation as his cue to address us all.

'Did I tell you about Ray?'

'Ray who?' I asked. I looked distinctly pale.

'I had a friend for years, since school really, called Ray. We would have a drink every week, sometimes less, but one day he seemed to disappear. I mean, he is the sort who might go off the map for a while, but not like this. For example, his wife disappeared off the face of the planet one day and he avoided me for a while. Then when I next saw him, he was a bit down on his luck and he'd moved somewhere awful in the Fens and he was a bit ashamed of it; he avoided me then, but not for long. But last week, I went round his house and he simply wasn't there, and the house looked unlived in. There was some post through the letter box. I don't know, it didn't feel right.'

'Have you reported him missing?' I asked.

'No not really. I mean, no.'

'What did he do?' I asked.

'He was a trucker. He used to run a company but that went under. When he became a trucker it seemed right somehow. He had the build for it, and he had a no nonsense attitude. I bet he fitted in well in that world. He certainly took to it easily enough, he soon learnt all about it and he would always have interesting tales to tell about the places he'd been to. I started to feel quite dull by comparison. He was always very cheerful, even when things went badly for him. He wasn't a moaner.'

'I'd heard he was a psychopath,' said someone else.

'This place really is a village, isn't it?' I said. I'd gone from pale to green.

'He used to collect news stories,' said Alan.

'What sort of news stories?'

'Like there was a theory that J Edgar Hoover was murdered by poisoned toilet paper.'

'Poisoned toilet paper?' asked Sean.

'Yeah, apparently you can put a chemical a bit like an insecticide onto toilet paper. It paralyses your breathing muscles and the strain on your heart makes you die of a heart attack. The beauty is that it takes a while to work, so after you've wiped it onto the mucous membrane of your arse, where it's easily absorbed, you then flush away the evidence.'

'Well there was definitely a CIA plot to give Castro exploding cigars,' said someone, 'so anything's possible.'

'I'd heard,' added Lisa, 'that the CIA tried to give Castro some poison that would make his beard fall out. Apparently having a beard was seen as a sign of virility.'

I spluttered loudly. 'That's it? This guy had been drinking with Alan all his life and we mention his loss briefly then get on with talking about the normal crap?'

Everyone looked at me as though I was mad.

When Chrissie and I had got home from the police station, she had asked me whether or not I had told them about the murder and I said no. She wasn't interested in my motives.

Picture her in the foreground distracted, going through her bag. Me behind, out of focus, pacing up and down, justifying myself. The story was too convoluted, I said. What plausible reason could I give for Ray having taken us hostage? Why such an assortment of people as Rick, Chris and I? The police would not be happy unless they saw a motive for us to be tied up; unless they saw a clear story whose veracity they could justify; to themselves, their colleagues, to a jury. The only way we could square the circle would be if we just made out Ray to be a lunatic.

Chrissie didn't listen to a word.

She said, 'Look Mike. I'm off. I think that's it really, eh? I'll see you.'

'Which means you won't see me,' I said. I hated that that was the last thing I said to her, but had no way to show it.

'I've been a lot of trouble,' she said.

It was only clear to me that she was going for good, because I knew her well.

She had a last look for stray belongings, then gave me a peck on the cheek .

I stood in the doorway of my house and she walked away along the pavement. She didn't look back.

Julio stood at the end of the church with Justine Dolly on his arm.

Beth was in her wheelchair in the pews with Mike. Julio started down the aisle. We began to hear laboured sounds of Beth's distressed breathing. It got louder and more rapid as Julio approached, echoing around the stone walls, a sound not unlike water going down a plughole only with a pulsing, painful quality.

As Julio drew exactly level, her breathing stopped all together as if inhaling and exhaling were now in deadlock, an impasse where neither would give ground. Julio's head turned to face her. Every eye in the church was on Beth. Her face was like stone. Her neck was pulsing and straining.

She spat at Julio.

A large mouthful of white spit landed on his cream coloured lapel. He looked down at it in horror.

Beth then pushed the lever of her wheelchair and went spinning forward attempting to knock him into the pews.

He sidestepped and Beth's chair got stuck against the seating.

'Stupid bitch,' cried Julio.

I woke up, relieved that it was a dream.

Less than three weeks until Chrissie's death and she'd never looked finer.

It was the wedding of the century. Matt Mann was to marry one Justine Dolly, spinster of this parish.

Justine had been temporarily disowned by her family for wanting to marry Matt. Her sisters had been forbidden to help her and this left her a bit short of potential bridesmaids. So in a surprise move they asked Chrissie, who gamely looked overjoyed.

Kindest of all, local philanthropist Julio Barrio put up the money for the wedding. He cut a deal with the vicar, no doubt, but it was still an amazing act of generosity. It would not go unreported in the Gazette.

It was all going so well. The danger with Matt is always that he'd have some idiot accident around his wedding day, so that he'd end up being pushed up the aisle in an iron lung, or something similar. But his stomach lacerations had healed well, the cast was off his arm; it was all looking good.

It was radiantly hot and a massive crowd of well-wishers gathered in the churchyard. The Poles all filed down the back of the church along with half the women from the carrot packing factory.

Chrissie looked great. This was a different Chrissie. Pure Audrey Hepburn. This was the Chrissie who lived in London a few years ago and who, when she returned to us, had been made larger by the experience. She wanted to be here with us, but she was bigger than us. She was Reapham's very own star.

Justine, the bride, had chosen a gown that involved mountains of fabric, scores of flowers and several veils. Christine on the other hand had gone for a Coco Chanel style. I felt love. If she'd worn sackcloth she would have been in danger of upstaging the bride, but either way, Justine was tickled pink. She loved it that her bridesmaid was so glamorous, it brought glamour to her.

Mike was a guest. In fact all the dental staff were there including Sue who sat with me. No Rick. Beth was in her wheelchair sat next to Mike.

Sue and I studiously avoided any conversation that involved death or burying bodies.

The bride was there before the groom. Half the town had camcorders. Justine and Chrissie posed by the gravestones and I took pictures for my paper.

Julio was giving Justine away. He'd broken out a new cream suit for the occasion. We took some pictures of them as a threesome.

I was just remarking to someone that Justine's family weren't going to turn up, but then next thing we knew there was a screech and the Dolly family Austin Allegro turned up and they all tumbled out.

Justine's father is a complete troglodyte. He emerged from the car blinking uneasily in the sunshine. He had a wife and two daughters who looked a lot like Justine.

Justine's father was full of himself.

'I told you that man was no good for you,' he said.

Justine avoided his gaze. Congenitally.

'Why?' I asked.

'Do you know what happened on the stag night?' he asked.

'Nothing. It was a week ago. It went fine.'

'No,' he said. 'Last night he went on someone else's stag night.'

This was news to us, but evidently the bush telegraph reaches the trog caves before us.

'All went well,' he continued, 'Although they got hopelessly drunk, and they piled back to some idiot's house. One of them decided to run a bath - who knows why - but because they were so drunk they put scalding hot water in it by mistake, right up to the top.'

'Matt then decided that he'd take off his clothes, run the length of the landing and dive in,' added a sister with a touch of Schadenfreude, 'Like it was a swimming pool.'

Another car drew up. Matt's father got out and scurried round to open the passenger door.

Matt got out. He had broken both arms: he had a cast from each shoulder going down to his elbows. From the elbows to the tips of his fingers he was blistered and pink and swollen. His forearms were twice their normal width. His fingers looked like ten plump carrots and were held dead ahead of him, presumably in the pose he must have been in when he hit the bath. His face, his entire head, was completely covered with white bandages. Someone had put a morning hat on top.

Justine's father made an ill-judged remark about Matt, and Matt's father flew at him. The two men, both tiny, had gripped each other's faces and were attempting to smack each other's heads on the gravestones.

A hundred camcorders whirred into action.

Someone tried to get the two fathers apart but only succeeded in giving Justine's father an advantage. He managed to send Matt's father spinning over a tomb - the kind that have a stone knight lying full length along the top of them. Matt's father was temporarily stunned. His head was on the knight's head. Justine's father climbed onto the grave to continue knocking the back of Matthew's skull against the stone nose of the knight.

There was a general sense that the men would be some time.

Julio told Matt to get into the church: he would be leading Justine down the aisle any moment.

Everyone was very nonchalant as Matt walked slowly down the aisle looking like something from The Curse of the Mummy.

The vicar led the service, hurrying a little because he had

another couple to marry at half past two and we were running late.

When the rings appeared, and the vicar suggested Matt put one on, a whispering went around as to how he would force it over his finger. Justine tried the ring finger, but it was too fat. She tried Matt's little finger but from somewhere inside the bandages there was a whimper. Justine was flapping. The eyes of Reapham were boring into her neck. Eventually she placed the ring between Matt's teeth.

'You may now kiss the bride,' said the vicar.

Everyone clapped and cheered as Justine, with her neck cricked down, attempted to find the gap in Matt's bandaging; her Pete Sampras tongue flailing in the still church air and then finally engaging with the white plaster slit which had the ring of gold protruding.

Beth had seemingly opted to behave herself in Julio's presence despite her well-publicised desire to murder him on sight, but as Julio walked back down the aisle the congregation seemed suddenly aware of her. There was a hush. People craned to see Beth's face.

'What?' she said. 'Look, I've grown as a person, alright?'

Mike found this very funny. He laughed for a few seconds and then somehow the rest of the congregation joined in.

At work, I was trying to get ahead. Trying to show the job the same respect that Julio seemed to be showing me these days.

Mike kept wandering in to sit with me. I'd barely spoken to him before Ray's death but now he came in all the time; I can only presume that he no longer had Chrissie to mull over his worries with. Here was a man who needed his problems shared.

'I keep waking up with a fresh panic,' he said. 'For example, that someone might have seen my car outside Ray's house.' He would say 'Ray' very softly.

He explained that he worried that sooner or later a relative would miss Ray and raise the alarm. He said sometimes he drove past the house just to see if there was a yellow police sign calling for witnesses to come forward.

Not once did Mike worry about Ray himself, or express sorrow; he would simply come in and ask if the police had notified my paper of a body being found. He had no idea that I'd buried the body. He couldn't even bring himself to ask about it. It was all very irritating.

For my part, I was worryingly relaxed about it all. Of course I wouldn't be so relaxed if the police were to make that call to our office and start taking an interest.

Mike's other line in conversation was Chrissie. He kept alluding to the fact that Chrissie had a drug problem. It really wasn't his place to tell me such things. Mike kept beating himself up that he'd never taken an interest. He didn't even know what drug she took. I think he kept imagining her somewhere on her own in a tatty room, going through hell drying herself out. The man had only a tentative grasp on reality.

I did a lot of soul searching about why I was so nonchalant. Perhaps it was a sign of *my* madness. Perhaps I really was the depressive with an alcohol problem that everyone took me for. A number of us depressives would welcome a catastrophe: it instantly takes the responsibility away of trying to do a good job of a normal life. Or perhaps it gives you something to struggle against, a real purpose in a so far directionless life.

Whatever the reason. Mike was shitting bricks and I wasn't.

MIKE

I popped in on Beth at one stage. She was alive and unrepentant after the wedding debacle.

Oddly enough Sue was sitting next to Beth drinking tea. She looked thunderstruck to see me.

'I'm coming in to work soon,' she said. 'Tomorrow.'

She started telling me how she didn't have a tumble dryer of her own and sometimes used Beth's. There was a new system where you could put solvents in the dryer and it acted like a dry cleaner and she was trying it.

'I tried it first recently and it worked so well I've started using it for everything,' she said.

I joked that presumably the deluxe pack went for the full dry cleaners experience; it told you it couldn't promise to get the stains out, intermittently lost items, and then charged you through the nose.

'I didn't know they did a deluxe pack,' replied Sue.

Sue mumbled something about returning to work the following Monday and scuttled off.

Beth looked pleased to see me but there was something in the air.

'So what's all this I hear?'

'What?' I replied.

'You and Chrissie calling it a day.'

'Oh that.'

'Look Mike,' said Beth, 'Christine likes you. You're good for her.'

'She doesn't think so. She never stops lying to me. I would forgive her anything, but she has to lie all the time.'

'Like what?'

'She didn't even tell me she was married.'

Beth smiled. 'You youngsters are funny.'

'How?'

'You've got no loyalty, no trust.'

'What?'

'Adam was quite a decent man. Christine married him young and it was a mistake. He wasn't terrible.'

I waited for more.

'He had lots of money and he was besotted with Christine so she married him. He didn't do anything wrong. She was at that stage where you imagine that despite everything you see around you, everything that happened to your parents, you'll be the one who'll make marriage work. A happy relationship that gives you everything you need.'

'So?' I asked.

'You'd be happier if she'd gone on and on about how awful her marriage was, told you endless details about it, or how she needed you? Instead she showed some loyalty to him. She's trying to sort out her life, she's trying to put some money together. She wants to avoid sponging off her husband or her father or you. She's trying to do it all with a bit of pride. You know, your generation are much happier when you're all moaning about each other.'

I thought about this for a while.

'Well,' I said, 'I'd have been happier if it had been her who'd told me this.'

'It matters to you who tells you a story?'

'You know, for an old woman, you're very astute,' I said.

'Less of the old. You probably wouldn't have believed her if she told you. You never trusted her, Mike, so there was little point in her telling you the truth.'

Beth had the air of someone who'd been waiting some time to tell me all this.

'Okay,' I joked, 'Say all that again and I'll take notes.'

DAVID

There was an air of festivity that September. Sue and I organised a drinking excuse to go into Cambridge. The gallery had stopped showing my cartoons after a week, but we thought we'd photo me outside the gallery anyway. Then we were going to photograph me standing by the counter of Watertone's buying my book.

As we say round here, 'Today I'm going to put on some clean socks and be somebody.'

Six of us sat in one of the new scrubbed floor bars that every city seems to boast these days.

Six of us shared a bottle of fizz which was the best we could afford.

We then went off to Watertone's. A friend of mine videoed me walking through the doors - okay, that sounds very pathetic, but at the time we thought it was fun. Then I was supposed to go to where my book was, dramatically pull one from the shelf, and be filmed paying for it.

In the foyer I went to the new releases section and checked alphabetically on the shelves, but I couldn't find my book. I then checked on the tables in that section, but I still couldn't find it.

We went up a floor to find the humour section. Every so often I turned dramatically on the stairs, smiling and beckoning to the camera, the way celebrities do in 'behind the scenes' footage; as if the act of going upstairs was, in itself, impressive.

I searched through the humour section and the cartoon book shelf. No joy there.

Eventually I went up to the tills and asked where I could find it.

The assistant was a pleasant woman in her early twenties. Probably a graduate, because obviously you'd need a degree to work in a book shop. She tapped at her computer for a while then looked pleased.

'We could order it for you,' she said.

'I already have a copy,' I replied.

The video camera seemed alarmingly close at that moment.

Neither the assistant nor I knew how to proceed. A queue was beginning to form behind me

I said, 'Okay, thanks.'

I had to endure a very slow journey home.

Julio wasn't surprised.

'A big book shop is stocking 50,000 titles or more,' he said, 'but there are over a million books in print. That's a one in twenty, one in thirty chance of you being stocked.'

I must have looked very defeated because Julio settled down next to me.

'We only got it published as a bit of a laugh,' said Julio. 'If it did well, that was lovely, but it wasn't very likely.'

I was taking this very hard.

'I think I've got this idea in my brain,' I said, 'that somehow I'm supposed to become famous sooner or later.'

'Ah, a common delusion in the young.'

'I think I almost saw it that I'd try and make this place famous in the same breath.'

Julio said, 'You'll get over it.'

'But you always seem to be trying to put Reapham on the map,' I said.

'Do I?' He sounded genuinely surprised at the notion.

I didn't want to accuse him again of faking the recent phenomena.

Julio picked up the baton. 'I don't think this part of the world feels comfortable being famous. I certainly don't think it's what everyone round here is about.'

Julio stopped for a while to collect his thoughts.

'You should see this place as a playground. No one bats an eyelid at what you do. I wouldn't live anywhere else in the world. I can wake up every morning of my life and my first thought is "How can I enjoy myself today?" It doesn't get better than that.'

'Yeah, I suppose so,' I said.

Julio changed his tone. He was very friendly. 'I've got something very fun, I might suggest to you in a day or so. You'll love it. I'll tell you about it. In a few days, okay?'

Julio left the room.

A few seconds later he popped his head round the door with a smile.

'You know, if a tree fell in a forest. It would make a sound, even if the London based media hadn't witnessed it.'

'Simply not true,' I replied.

MIKE

I started stalking Chrissie's house.

I rang up Beth, but she wouldn't give me Chrissie's land line number.

I'd ring Chrissie's mobile phone but I would always get the a message service.

'Hi, it's Mike,' I'd say, 'just saying hello.'

One Saturday morning I sat in my car ten yards down the road from her house and just waited. But the hours went by, and I'd read the same paper four times.

I saw the door open, so I hurriedly got out of the car and walked towards their house, but it was Adam. It was now too late to go back.

'Hi,' I said. 'Is Chrissie in?'

'Chrissie?' he asked. He sounded puzzled.

'Your wife. I'm a friend of your wife's.'

'Yes, I know.' He scrutinised me. 'She doesn't live here any more.'

'Oh,' I said.

'Er sorry,' he added. It wasn't clear what he was sorry about.

'Has she got a new address?'

'Probably,' he replied. 'Sorry, she asked me not to give it

out. If I see her, I could pass on a message. You're..?'
   'Mike.'
   'Mike, right.'
   'No message,' I said.
   He smiled. He had a kind face. He started to walk away.
   'Have you tried her mobile?' he shouted over his shoulder.
   'I'll do that,' I said.

DAVID

Sue and I bumped into Chrissie in Reapham. She was outside a pub and called across to us. We sat down and had a drink with her. It was one of the last summer evenings. The other tables were quite busy. There was no doubt that Reapham phenomena had led to a number of quite normal people popping out to us to have a look at the area.

Chrissie looked very well and happy. Not only was she the only person who seemed comfortable talking about what happened, she jumped straight in with it.

'Do you think anyone's going to want Ray's house?' she asked.

'What?'

'Ray's house. It's just sitting there dormant.'

'You can't have his house,' said Sue, 'That's sick.'

'No. Shooting him's sick. Living in a house that no one else seems to want or claim, that's common sense.'

I couldn't believe my ears.

'Isn't that against the law?' I asked.

'I doubt it. It's just squatting. If someone asked me to leave, I could always leave.'

'You get all that joyriding up that end of the common,' said Sue.

'Oh come on you guys, I'm not really going to do it,' she

said. She started cross examining Sue about Ricky, but was stonewalled. It's not often Sue resents telling people about her life. Sue, with an air of getting her own back, cross-examined Chrissie about Mike.

'Oh, I'm thinking of offering him a new arrangement,' she said.

'How do you mean?' I asked.

'I think I need a sort of partial deal. Perhaps from Friday evening through to Monday morning we live together at his place and the rest of the week is my own. If he wants to see me during the week he has to ask. If we want to do something separate during a weekend, we have to ask. What do you think?'

'Why don't you just move in?' asked Sue.

'With Mike? I could do. I do love him. I really love him, you know? But we keep tripping up. So I think this partial deal could work. I could really try hard for the two or three days. Mike deserves it. He's very sweet to me.'

'I can't see it myself,' said Sue, 'But I suppose he is my boss.'

'Well he's very good at sex' said Chrissie. 'You know, real dangerous sex.'

'Really??' I said.

'No, not really,' she said. 'But he likes to be thought of as dangerous, on the edge. You know, it might make him happy to put these things about...'

Sue was red now. She pretended to find something down the High Street fascinating.

'His friends are pretty irritating,' I said, 'I mean all that film stuff; you're just quoting someone else's imagination all the time. It's like endlessly telling other people's jokes.'

'Yeah, but I love him.' She sort of shook her head. 'Yeah, his friends are a drag. Anyway I've just come out of a relationship so I ought to be careful moving into something else.'

'So you've suggested this part-time arrangement to Mike?' I asked.

'No. Well we're not speaking at the moment. But, you know, I'm hoping to get the guts up to do it.'

I'd finally had my car sorted out and gave Sue a lift home.

We got as far as Sanity Row but had to turn back because the joy riders seemed to be out early. We went the other way and Sue invited me in for a cup of tea. We were just settling down when there was a knock on the door.

On the doorstep was Julio. He was surprised to see me.

'Is Ricky here?' he asked.

'No. Do come in though,' I replied.

Sue fussed around trying to find a beer for Julio. She's not much of a drinker so she ended up making him a cup of tea, then panicked that perhaps an Italian would prefer coffee.

Julio made a bit of small talk. For the first time ever, he was edgy.

He said, 'David, do you mind if I have a word with Sue alone?'

'I'd prefer it if you stayed,' said Sue.

Julio looked uncertain, then shrugged.

'I need to contact Rick,' he said, 'have you any idea if he'll be back this evening?'

'Actually, I don't know if he'll be in tonight,' said Sue. Sue was lying. She knew she probably wouldn't see Rick at all.

'You see,' he went on, 'I've knocked on the door a few times here and he's not been in, so I just wondered...'

'I can get him to ring you.'

'No it's alright. It's about money really. When he was working at the garage we had a little pension scheme and we never got notified of another scheme when he left us.'

'I don't follow you,' said Sue.

'Effectively, we owe him a bit of money from the fund. We need to transfer it, or have his signatures to keep doing what we're doing. It's quite important we get a signature quite soon. It's our fault; we let things lapse and now we're in a bit of a hurry.'

This story was such bullshit, and Sue's reaction to Julio was intriguing. Julio got a notebook out. His hand was shaking a little.

'Look,' he said, 'I just need a few ideas as to where I could find him.'

Sue sat and looked at him for ages but didn't say anything. Then she relented and came out with lots of details of where he might be found: friends and places where he sometimes did odds and ends of work. Sue looked rattled as she told him these things.

Julio figured he'd got as much as he could hope for, and left.

'What was that about?' I asked Sue.

'I have no idea,' she said. She looked as though she were lying.

MIKE

A newspaper swirls anticlockwise, its print a blur. It spins closer towards us and slows until we can read it.

The headline was, 'Do As I Say Or I Open The Kitty.'

'A woman from Reapham faced magistrates today charged with holding up a supermarket. Christine Hedges, 27, of North Fen Common, Reapham was found guilty of...'

There followed lots of puns like 'cat burglar' and 'she was caught by a whisker.'

Chrissie was quoted half way down as saying, 'I was hungry; I needed some clothes; you know how it is.' The penultimate paragraph told us that she had received a fine, and the final paragraph said that the cat had appeared to have made a 'purrfect' recovery from its ordeal.

I walked into the staff room. The nurses stifled their giggles. I surveyed them for a while then insisted Emma handed over the newspaper she was now sitting on.

Sue was in the staff room. I took her out to have a word. She was very nervous.

'Sue, tell me,' I said, 'in the house that Ray... in Ray's house.'

'Yes?'

'Did you see any syringe or anything?'

'Syringe?'

'There was a little box made up of a few syringes and stuff.'

'There might have been a box, why?'

'But you don't know what happened to it?'

'No,' she said.

I took myself to Sanity Row. I stood for a ridiculously long time outside Ray's front door. I went to knock, then stopped myself.

I mumbled to myself, 'there's no law against knocking on a door. I can say I'm looking for a patient.'

I went to knock again, but the door opened and I jumped a mile.

'Jesus wept Chrissie, what are you doing here?'

'Oh this and that. What about you?' she said brightly.

I was stunned. I whispered, 'Are the police with you?'

'Why would the police be with me?'

I noticed she was holding a sink plunger. 'Do you know anything about blocked drains?' she asked. 'I can't get the water to drain away.'

'You're living here?' I asked. 'How can you live here after that man was killed here?'

'Well of course I don't remember that because of that drug I'd had. It makes it easier.'

I just stared, then absentmindedly added, 'You haven't got mains drainage here, have you? You've got soakaways, septic tanks.'

Chrissie raised an eyebrow. 'Ah,' she said, 'I didn't know that. Do you think it makes a difference?'

'It means you can't use bleach for a start,' I said. 'I was looking for a box I left. It had syringes and stuff in it.'

'Yeah, I threw it away.'

'How?'

'I put it in the bin.'
'You're not allowed to put syringes in a normal bin,' I said.
Chrissie rolled her eyes.
'Well, that's what I did,' she said.
'Right. Um, could you come outside a second?' I said.
'Why?'
'Because I don't want to go in the house.'
Chrissie started laughing. 'Whatever,' she said.
'Chrissie, I love you.'
'I know you do.'
'I went through a lot of shit for you,' I said.
'What? What did you go through? You've always got one foot out of the boat Mike.'
'I could have died. The fucker was shooting at me.'
She smirked. 'Well there is that,' she said. 'But then I don't remember that either. Ricky's a prat, isn't he?'
'That's all you have to say?'
'Mike, this is your big chance to win me back, and frankly, you're just getting ratty.'
I shook my head in disbelief. I looked down Sanity Row to see if anyone was witnessing us.
Chrissie started getting chatty. 'You know,' she said, 'The funny thing was that Rick wasn't as manic as you'd think. I mean, he'd lost the package, and he's a psycho at heart, but he just...'
'What?'
'Well don't you think it's odd? When we first came across Rick by the truck, he didn't put much pressure on Ray. He was just kind of going through the motions, don't you think? If anything he was just pleased to make a clean escape.'
'So?'
'So he must have been alone there when that truck first turned up. We were late because of Matt's breakdown. Rick

had every chance to take whatever it was and try and blame us. Ray's the perfect scapegoat now he's dead. Rick had to be seen to go to endless trouble to get Ray to tell him where the stuff was; he had to rifle through Ray's house and take his truck to get some of the money back, but let's face it in reality he might have had it all along.'

'Well it's all done and dusted now,' I said.

'Yeah, but Rick's probably got whatever it is.'

'Don't even go there, Chrissie. Forget it.'

Chrissie started laughing. We were getting on well.

She leant forward to me and said, 'We'll think of something.'

It wasn't clear what she was referring to, but it seemed like a good sign.

'I've left Adam,' she said.

'Oh?' I said.

She went to touch me, then withdrew her hand again.

'I'm really sorry about everything I've done,' I said.

'Oh that's okay.'

'No, I'm not sorry,' I said. 'This is stupid. You've not played fair with me and...'

Chrissie looked chastened, demoralised. She looked down, away from me.

'Yeah, I know,' she said. 'Look perhaps we can meet and talk some time, eh?'

'Yeah,' I said.

DAVID

The state of my house had got completely out of control. I made a tactical retreat taking a few of my belongings and pleaded with Sue to stop at her place for a while. The plan was that I would return refreshed, launch a surprise attack one day; my own little D Day.

I arrived at Sue's feeling that I had even fewer core belongings than when I was a student, but at least that prevented it from looking as if I was moving in for good.

Sue and I celebrated with a good old fashioned cup of tea - a bit of a theme at her place - then we mulched in front of the TV.

I was to sleep on Sue's sofa that night with the life sized china pierrot leaning over me all night offering me an ash tray. The cushions of the sofa stank of cigarettes, presumably from when Rick lived there. It was so at odds with Sue's obsessive cleanliness.

I smiled to myself that I'd somehow ended up on Sanity Row. Along with the Gnome family who've got this garden full of gnomes, front and back. If you visit them in the winter, they've taken them all inside and all these dorky gnomes are sitting all over the carpet and the settees. The family have to stand.

And there's Bob, who turfed his wife out when he got another womnan, but she refused to go, so he waited till market day and she was out, and he had all the windows removed. Apparently he'd checked legally he was allowed to do it, or asked everyone down the pub and they'd agreed. So Margaret spent a defiant night huddled in the house. Almost instantly, he fell out with this new woman, so Bob and his wife are forced to live in the coldest house in Christendom because they're having trouble getting the frames back in.

And there's me and Sue.

Sanity Row folks. Evidently my spiritual home.

I was woken up by a commotion somewhere outside and when I went to have a look there seemed to be a bit of a glow in the sky as though there was a bonfire somewhere.

I went upstairs and I could see that there was a car on fire further down the Row. Orange flames were leaping up in the dark and there was smoke and lots of people outside watching it. I spent a fair time gazing at it and then went back to my sofa.

I woke up a second time with someone banging loudly on the door. This wasn't a very restful house. When I came to fully, I realised I could hear Rick shouting for Sue. He sounded very desperate.

There was long pause, and I was so tired that for a second I thought I'd dreamt it, but then he shouted again. He was beating and pounding the door but I just lay there for what felt like forever. The pounding stopped and there was a rustle of a key being used in the lock. Then the knocking started again.

I realised that Sue was now in the room with me. She had crept in silently. She knelt by me in the darkness and held my hand.

Rick shouted again and banged on the door. I squeezed Sue's hand. We waited.

Rick shouted and banged again.

'Sue. Open up Sue. For the love of God open up.'

It was louder this time but shorter. Then there was a silence.

239

We waited and waited but that was it.

We didn't dare move for an eternity. I fell asleep before Sue had even gone back upstairs.

The next morning I went, in my role as local reporter, to see what had happened in Sanity Row the previous night. I was several days away from my deadline so I was in no hurry.

I knocked on a few doors, but no one was there. There were two burned out vehicles. One looked like a VW Polo, the other a Ford. I drove back via the bypass. The mystic traveller folk had diminished in numbers now but were still in evidence. Perhaps they hang around somewhere like this until some other occurrence happens somewhere else in the country, or they get moved on by the police.

While driving, I got a phone call from my office. I was told Anglia News was running stories about Sanity Row on TV. Sue's house was nearer than the office, so I rushed back there.

And then, there it was. My chest tightened as I watched the news item. A body had been found in the Fens. There was no head or hands to identify the body, but there were witnesses who think they saw the murder. Evidently a man had been chained up behind a Range Rover and was dragged along some of the local roads. The body that was found had huge amounts of its skin missing and the police thought that it was probably the same body.

A reporter talked to camera, standing outside the police station in Cambridge. Police weren't sure if this death tied in with a second death on the same night.

An asylum seeker had been murdered. He apparently had managed to escape from the Immigration Centre but was picked up by some local youths thought to be joy riding. It is unclear whether the immigrant was coerced into the car or felt he was getting a lift to freedom.

The youths took him to Sanity Row, let him free then chased him with cars, knocking him over and killing him.

Over and above this there were eye witness reports of another incident during the same evening where a man had been seen being chased along Sanity Row by some people in a car.

Witnesses said that a man had tried to get in to one or two houses and then had run down to the area where the youths were joyriding. He'd run straight across the old munitions road and a car had clipped him and sent him flying. The people following him then bundled him into their car and sped away. It was unclear which, if either, of the victims this was.

After lunch I went out and bought an Evening News. I felt self-conscious even buying it. Walking away from the paper shop it seemed as if even the act of reading the relevant story would somehow draw attention to me. The Evening News very much said the same as Anglia TV but it added that the headless body had the remnants of bandages on his legs and had wounds that appeared to predate his death.

The article further went on to say that no one had come forward to identify either body, that one of them was thought to be to do with local criminal gangs settling scores, and that the Immigration Centre had stepped up security.

The police were quoted as saying that there was no reason for the population to be alarmed.

Rick's death had left me with few emotions I could put my finger on. Consciously I didn't think much about him, possibly because I hadn't actually seen him that night. The nearest I had to a visual image was my view of the door that he was knocking on. I could imagine him being clipped by a car, I could see that in my mind, but I didn't dwell on it.

But I noticed other things about myself. I had a general blankness about me, a loss of spirit. Paradoxically that meant I got on very well with my work without feeling the need for distractions. Despite this blankness, I found I was unduly ratty with other people.

Julio came into my office with a half-arsed story for me and I bit his head off.

He was taken aback.

'I'll take it to one of your colleagues if you like,' he said.

'Do that,' I said. This was my benefactor I was talking to: the generous purveyor of exhibitions and weddings.

'What is your problem David?'

'What's my problem? What's my problem??' I was getting shrill. I had no idea what my problem was. I heard myself saying, 'Look I'm just a stooge. You don't let me in to what's going on, you just expect me to toe the line and dutifully do your bidding.'

'I think that is a basic premis of the employer/employee relationship,' said Julio.

'Yes!' I shouted. 'I know!' It was as stupid as it sounds.

We had a stand-off.

'What exactly did you want to know?' he said finally.

'How did you get that gravity defying hill sorted out?' My English was deserting me.

'What's your theory?' he asked. 'I'd heard that you'd been getting truckers to move stuff up from Spain.'

'It wasn't me directly,' he said, 'but I had organised some transport of rocks.'

'Why?'

'You're going to laugh, because it is truly crazy looking back. Have you ever heard of the Gerona Miracle?'

'No.'

'There is a road in the foothills of the Pyrenees where vehicles appear to freewheel uphill. It's magnetic or something.'

I laughed. 'You're telling me you shipped the rocks from there to Reapham to try and duplicate it and created a magnetic hill? That's crazy.'

'No. We needed the truck to go from Spain to here anyway.' He stopped himself. 'Don't you ever have whims, David? I thought it might be magical.' He stopped. 'No. hang on, you tell me. Why wouldn't it work?'

I shrugged. 'It's still crazy. So what *did* you do?'

'I had to have my car doctored to run without apparent assistance. Everyone was so busy checking the hill, it didn't occur to them to check the car. And you'd have to be pretty mad to tinker with a Ferrari.'

I was incredulous. 'Why?'

'Oh why this, why that? It only cost a few grand. I made that up easily on rent to the hippies who turned up, and the trade at the pubs.' He looked at me in a disappointed manner. 'You know I swear I'm the only person around here who knows how to have some fun.'

I was all spent.

Julio pointed to the paper he was holding. 'Do you want this story or not?'

'Yeah, sure,' I said.

Julio walked out of the office. About a minute later he returned.

'I'll tell you what,' he said, 'it might be time to let you into that idea I've had.'

It was with considerable unease that I let Julio into my house.

'Don't we need petrol or something?' I asked.

'Definitely not,' said Julio. 'It's got to look like an accident. It's why God created gas cookers. The police only think it's arson if the fire is started in more than one place at the same time. Where is your cooker?'

We were standing in the kitchen doorway but it was still a fair question.

'I'm sure the cooker's in here somewhere,' I joked.

My landlord found this oddly unamusing. The carpet chose this moment to slop under foot.

'Do you walk around this place in your bare feet?' he asked.

'Never,' I reassured him.

He nodded approvingly.

Julio took a clean white handkerchief out of his top pocket and gingerly pushed the kitchen door to be as open as possible. He barely needed to touch it before it was sucked backwards; the debris stacked behind drawing it in with gluing arms. On the other side of the kitchen there was a gurgling of gas through fluid from deep within a bin sack. Julio and I gripped each other's shoulders and crept further in, our necks tensing away from what was in front of us.

The front of the cooker had cardboard boxes pushed against it. These appeared to be full of half filled bags and newspapers. The top of the cooker was apparently a centimetre deep in ghee. Julio and I had our heads leaned together, each hoping the other would summon up the courage to do something. I extended a foot to try and stir things away from the oven.

The gas knobs themselves were hidden behind some crumpled carrier bags. I stretched out a couple of fingers, pincer like. The bottom of the bags appeared to have a liquid in them where something like fruit had rotted. This swilled when I moved it to give a pendulum effect; slower than you'd think because the liquid had an unnatural viscosity. As if to confirm that we were now in some alternative reality, the top of the bags weren't wet at all; they were hardened and spot-welded to the gas knobs.

'I guess we need to turn one of the knobs and lean something innocent against it to keep it on,' I said.

'Won't that activate the sparking device that lights the gas,' asked Julio.

I giggled, but tried to look guilty. 'The cooker is far too dirty for that to work.'

'Okay, well first let's rig up the lamp in the hall.'

We'd got an old desk lamp and a timer to plug in. Our bright idea was that we'd rig it up just as you would if you were going away and wanted to ward off burglars. The difference being that we'd got an old lamp and roughed it up a bit so that it had some threadbare electric wire that would create a nice spark.

We rigged it up in the hall to go off at 6pm. 'What if it doesn't work?' I asked.

'Then you run up a large gas bill,' said Julio.

MIKE

Sue and I were driving on the edge of town. It was darker and more autumnal than before. There were bronzed leaves ankle deep by the side of the road.

Sue was chatting ten to the dozen about the new road they were finally making for Sanity Row. She was very pleased with it. The authorities had started taking an interest in the area and they were spending money putting it legally on the map.

'How's Rick?' I asked.

'Oh I don't see much of him these days,' she replied.

I looked over at Sue.

'How pregnant are you now?' I asked.

Sue flushed a little.

'I'm not sure of my dates yet,' she said. 'When I have my scan it might be clearer.'

I stopped the car outside a new building. A nursing home. The adjoining property was an old shop called Arkwrights. They appeared to be boarding it up.

We were taken into the day room and told to wait. There was a old woman there I recognised.

I whispered to Sue, 'Didn't she used to be the woman who walked the streets wearing black bin sacks and crapping on the pavements?'

Sue nodded.

She was sitting asleep in a floral cotton dress and slippers. Her head was thrown back, and every minute or so her denture would fall down and her tongue would push it up again, without her apparently waking.

'She's dreaming, no doubt, of her glory days, defecating on the pavements of Reapham,' I said.

Sue sighed and started unpacking our dental equipment from a bag.

The television was on too loud. It looked like Jerry Springer, but in fact it was Anglia TV: the programme had been made in the area. The caption, 'My Life Is Ruined By My Stepdaughter' was at the foot of the screen. A teenager was dishing the dirt on her family but was in tears as she, in turn, was being humiliated live on television. The old people in the home were oblivious to it all. They were too out of it, or too frail to get up and change channel. There was a liquid crystal display sellotaped to the wall of the day room. It read '82. Too Hot.'

There was a movement in the doorway. A teenage helper with a wayward bra strap was helping an old woman towards us. The woman was tiny, she insisted on walking herself but was too frail. The teenager grew slightly impatient. Instead of helping the woman, she was now dragging her.

'We've got four patients to see, I believe,' I said. I found the list for the helper to look at.

When we left the premises it was dark. I told Sue I'd drop her home and we drove through narrow unlit back routes.

I had to swerve the car to avoid a ship's cannon that some idiot had placed at the side of the track. She told me it was some eccentric who placed his cannon to either face the Russians or the Middle East depending on his view of foreign affairs at any given moment. It was angled such that if he was defending us from the Russians, you had to drive to the left of it, but otherwise you had to drive to the right.

'A lot of cars bump into it,' she said.

'That's a story to tell them in Cambridge,' I said.

I focussed on a bright light in the sky about a mile away. It seemed to be flashing.

'What do you reckon that is?' I asked Sue.

'Oh don't ask,' she replied.

'No really, what is it?'

'It's a UFO. It's a genuine real McCoy UFO.'

'How do you know?' I asked.

'Because Julio and David have organised it.'

I waited for more.

'There's a town in Devizes, or called Devizes or something, where they had all these crop circles and stuff and Julio discovered that it boosted local tourism by 500% or something stupid, so every eight weeks or so he's going to stage some sort of event.'

'You're kidding me?'

'If only. Everyone knows about it, but that doesn't seem to make a difference. They've got themselves a crop duster and covered it with swirly lights, and Matt's got the video camera at the ready.'

We watched for a while. It was wet and windy. We couldn't hear that it was a plane.

'David's finally gone native,' I said.

'He is a native,' said Sue.

'Yeah, I know,' I said quietly.

We watched as the light moved to the right and turned swiftly and flew away from us.

'I admire it really,' I said.

'It's incredibly stupid,' said Sue. 'Still, you can't hear that it's a plane. They chose a windy night that was very dark so that people wouldn't cotton on.'

'No one's going to swallow it are they?'

'I'm not sure that's the point is it?' she shrugged.

There was an explosion somewhere in the distance.

'What's that?' I asked.

'They've decided to set fire to the house David lives in. I very much doubt that will be enough to kill off the cockroaches and vermin that live there, but it's worth a try.'

'Why would they want to burn it down?'

'It's falling down anyway. It's listed and would cost too much to do up.'

'I'm amazed insurance companies put up with Julio,' I said.

'Yeah, so am I.'

'When they say you're only allowed one phone call,' said Chrissie, 'it's complete crap. They've let me keep my mobile.'

'Where are you ringing from?' I asked.

'The police station. Mike, they're questioning me on suspicion of murder. Do you know a solicitor or anything? On TV, people always seem to already have a solicitor they can call for just such contingencies, but frankly...'

Chrissie gave me contact details and I put the phone down.

I rang Lisa.

'Lisa, you're a solicitor...'

I sat in the same police station corridor as before. At length Lisa appeared and sat down with me.

'Do you think Chrissie could kill someone?' she asked.

'I wouldn't have thought so,' I replied.

Lisa pushed a pen around her pad. It didn't make a mark.

'What do you know about the house where she lives. Has she been there long?'

'What do you mean?' I asked.

'I mean what I say.' Lisa looked at me puzzled.

'She hasn't been there long,' I said.

'There is compelling evidence that a murder was committed on that premises.'

I tried to look matter of fact.

'Well she hasn't been there that long,' I said.

'How long?'

'The previous guy left in a hurry, I hear.'

'But she bought the house off him?' said Lisa. 'I mean it does seem far-fetched that Chrissie murdered the man and then started living in his house.'

'Yes, that is far-fetched,' I said.

'I asked Chrissie about buying the house, and she seemed a bit vague.'

'Well it must be quite a shock to be interviewed as a murder suspect.'

'Precisely,' said Lisa, 'and obviously there'll be proof if you've bought a house.'

'Ah,' I said, 'not in Sanity Row.'

Sue had been bursting to tell me something for a long time. She was restless but also clearly pleased with herself.

One Saturday morning out of the blue, she said, 'I've got something I want to show you.'

She got some rubber gloves out of the kitchen draw and beckoned me into the garden.

She took a small trowel and after many comedy looks over her shoulder to check that she wasn't being watched - the garden is not overlooked so presumably she was checking that a block of flats hadn't sprang up over night – started digging.

Where the patio met the garden there was a little gulley covered in leaves. Sue soon came up with a package about six inches by half and inch.

'I'm pretty sure they're diamonds,' said Sue.

'Where did you get them?' I asked.

'In the house,' she replied, as if this were somehow natural.

'You had a packet of diamonds hanging around the house?' Needless to say we were whispering.

'No,' said Sue. 'I was cleaning around the house, and I've got in the habit of checking nooks and crannies after that time the police raided the place, and you know what Rick's like.'

'Sue, get to the point. Where did you find these diamonds? And when?'

'Behind the sink in the bathroom. Weeks ago.'

I was praying I wouldn't need the long version of Sue's story. I tried to dream up a good supplementary question. Sue continued anyway.

'When I found them I just knew I had to move them. And I was right. I came home one evening and I had this feeling that everything had been moved. I just knew that someone had been in the house. I couldn't put my finger on it. There was a magazine on the table that wasn't quite how I put it and in my bedroom there was a drawer that wasn't closed properly and when I looked it was because the clothes weren't flattened properly.'

'Yeah, I get it.'

'It's horrible to think someone was in my bedroom. And then James Palmos came to see me. You know, the guy Rick sometimes works for and he was looking for Rick just like Julio was that time. You see, when I'm here I can bolt and chain the doors, but when I'm out Rick has got keys and can get in, so I bet he was able to hide the stuff.'

During this conversation I had opened the package carefully. Just seeing the first couple of diamonds made me freeze and repackage them. Paranoia swept through me. I, too, was now scanning the horizon for imaginary tower blocks. 'I think we've got to hand them in,' I said, 'or hand them back.'

'No. I want them,' said Sue.

'We're way out of our depth Sue. We wouldn't know how to fence them. This could go horribly wrong.'

I gave a furtive look left and right and then crossed the road. The street looked particularly grey; there was evidence of rain on the pavements.

I all but pulled my collar over my head to hide my face as I entered the prison.

Chrissie had the mannerisms of cheerfulness but looked drawn and frightened.

'I think me having a criminal record was a clincher,' she said.

'What's their actual proof?' I asked. 'Did someone tip them off?'

'I did!' said Chrissie.

'What?'

'The drains were blocked so I got a man in and he recommended we drained the septic tank. I might have thought twice about it if someone had told me. Apparently the tank was full of evidence of a murder.'

'Really? How?'

'No idea.'

'Christ,' I said. 'You really shouldn't have moved into that house.'

'Yeah well I'm beginning to see that.' There was an edge of hysteria to her now.

'Fuck. So what are you going to do?' I asked.

'Deny everything and hope for the best.'

'Okay, what can I do?'

'Well,' she said, leaning closer, 'If you could witness that I bought the house fair and square, you know, witness me signing stuff.'

I looked uncertain. 'You'd need to present a document, and for that it would have to have Ray's signature on it.'

'Surely you could come up with something Mike. I mean, if they just think I moved in, it'll look awful.'

'Yes, but I'm really not sure...'

Chrissie had lost what little colour was left in her face.

'Chrissie, I will do everything I can.'

'But you won't will you, Mike?' Chrissie started crying; she was annoyed with herself for doing so.

'Chrissie, I will do everything I can.'

'Oh Jesus. Oh Jesus. Okay Mike. Okay Mike, forget it. We're going to have to forget it.'

DAVID

'Julio,' I said, 'I've made a bit of a discovery. I think we may have something that you're looking for.'

'Really?' asked Julio.

I told him about the diamonds. He was very attentive, listening silently to what I had to say. For some reason I was expecting him to get cross, but it never happened.

He thought for a while, and said, 'Who else knows this?'

'No one. Just Sue and I.'

'Keep it that way. I'm serious. Not one person. Not a parent, not a girlfriend, no one. Those are not my diamonds. But if we are very cautious, very slow, then at some stage in the future we can sell them.'

We.

Sue was in my office almost instantly, as though she had some psychic link or telescope from across the road.

I explained the situation.

Instead of dancing round the room she simply asked, 'How much are they worth?'

'No doubt Julio will rip us off, not least because I think he's lying.'

'In what way?' asked Sue. 'Coming to think of it, you always think everyone's lying.'

'I think they're his diamonds. At least in part. Nothing I could put my finger on, just something about the way he looked.'

'How much do we get?' asked Sue.

'Tens of thousands of pounds. Each. But we have got to shut up about this.'

Sue sat quietly looking at the floor. A smile kept coming in pulses.

'There's something else I want to talk to you about,' she said. 'Look. We're friends, yeah?'

'Yes,' I said. It sounded grave.

'David, I hate living on my own. You have no idea. But look, I don't want a relationship or anything. I just wondered if you'd like to share my house. You know. Like living together but not living together. I've got a spare room and everything, at least I will have when I've got Rick's stupid bits of motorbike out of it. And we need to get a bed and stuff.' Sue was very nervous. 'I realise now that I'm not someone who can live alone, but to be honest, I don't think you should either.'

'You might well be right,' I said.

'Well?'

'I'd love to share a house with you Sue.'

Sue hugged me. She was thrilled.

MIKE

I was slaving over a hot patient and there was a knock on my door. Emma appeared and beckoned to me to come close.

'The police want to have a word with you. It's about the murder on Sanity Row.'

I apologised to the patient and made my way towards the waiting PCs. I greeted them both by name. They waited until I was close before speaking.

'We wondered if we could question you in connection with a local murder investigation?'

'Okay,' I said, sitting down carefully.

'We appreciate it is a sensitive matter in a close-knit community like this, so I think it is in everyone's interest for this to be as low key as possible.'

'Okay,' I said again.

'We were wondering therefore if you could identify the deceased for us by their dental records.'

'What?' I asked.

'We have found a skull and a jaw bone at the site in question and the forensic scientist has made a note of the fillings and so forth in the teeth.'

'But we didn't treat Ray Renard,' I said, 'so we wouldn't have any notes.'

The policeman looked puzzled for a while.

'No, you misunderstand, the bones found are thought to be those of a woman. It is possible that they were those of Mr Renard's wife. His daughter says that she used to be treated here.'

I still looked very ill, but managed to say, 'Really? I'll check. What was her first name?'

A slow tracking shot down the length of the table. An abundance of vividly coloured food; some steaming and untouched, some being spooned onto plates. Claret is being poured into glasses. There is a general sense that time has passed.

We know all the faces: Lisa, Alan, all the gang are there. They are very animated. There seems to be more than one conversation going on.

'I suppose her cut-off attitude could have been a sign of depression,' said Sean.

'I thought she just didn't like us,' said Lisa.

At the other end of the table Alan was saying, 'So when they analysed the bones it was actually the bones of Ray's wife. He'd murdered her and as far as they can work out he chopped her up and flushed her down the drains.'

'Jesus. Where is he now?' asked Gabby.

'The best guess is he sold his house for what he could and took off in his truck,' I said. 'His truck hasn't been seen since.'

'The amazing thing,' said Alan, 'was that he'd been telling us one way or another that he'd murdered her.'

'How?' asked Gabby.

'Well in stories,' said Alan. He got stuck how to explain.

I said, 'A lot of people have now come forward to say that Ray spent several months hinting at all this. He would talk about similar stories in the press; he would go to the police about nothing in particular, he would even ask them to search his house on some pretext or other; as if he wanted to get caught.'

'It seems that Jean made the mistake of knocking on his door one day down at Sanity Row,' said Alan, 'just to see how he was. Ray just flipped and somehow murdered her. By chance, no one knew where she was that day and Ray got away with it.'

Helen reached behind her to the pile of papers. She sorted through them and passed them around. Some were local papers, some were nationals.

Sean had a knee up on the table. He was forking food into his mouth as he read one of the papers. 'The press was fair to everyone. To Chrissie, to this Ray chap.' he said, a bolus of food clearly visible.

Lisa touched me on the sleeve. 'So how had Chrissie seemed when you saw her?'

I donned a resigned, 'what can you do?' look. 'I mean, obviously she looked nervous,' I said. 'At that stage they hadn't worked out that it was Ray's wife they'd found. They'd still charged her with murdering Ray.'

Everyone had gone quiet to listen to me.

'So she was subdued, upset. I mean, obviously,' I continued. 'She thought they were still going to prosecute her. And then there was also the on-off drug thing.'

'Let's face it,' said Lisa, 'she must have been very desperate to have moved into that ghastly house in the first place.'

'Well I always liked her,' said Sean. He then looked worried he'd said the wrong thing. 'There's only so much you could have done, Mike. You'd taken knock after knock. When you've had that many knocks you don't tend to get a happy ending. People lose interest in going that extra mile for the other person.'

Everyone agreed on that.

There's a long unflinching close up on my face. Unblinking.

I look older. My eyes look directly into the camera. We wait. There's still no movement. My pupils dart down briefly then return. This is the end, but we're still having to wait. I nod imperceptibly.

It's over.

THE EVENING NEWS 2ND NOVEMBER.

THREE PRISONERS KILL THEMSELVES DURING WEEK

Three prisoners, two of them on suicide watch, were found hanging in their cells during the last week, reviving concerns about the care of vulnerable inmates.

The co-director of Inquest, a group concerned about deaths in custody, said that she feared prison service guidelines were still not being implemented properly.

Prison staff found Miss Christine Hedges, 29, hanging in Halterbeach prison on Saturday afternoon and were unable to resuscitate her. She shared a cell but hanged herself while her cellmate was out on the wing. She was being held on remand on murder charges.

Jamie Rowan, 24, who was serving an eight month sentence for driving while disqualified and theft, was found hanging in his cell at Hull on Wednesday, the same day that Norwich prison announced the death of David Gleeson.

The deaths bring the total number of prisoners who have died in custody to 70 this year. A spokeswoman for the prison service said it was not unusual to see a cluster of deaths at this time of year.

But Daniela Frost of Inquest said: "There's no doubt that the prison service has invested a lot of resources in the problem, but the reality is that far too often the deaths raise questions about the implementation of suicide prevention guidelines."

The episode is a further blow for the Halterbeach Centre which has received extensive media interest following a series of allegations of staff brutality last year.

Police say they do not feel there were any suspicious circumstances surrounding Miss Hedges' death and will not be investigating further.